SNOWED

A RYLIE COOPER MYSTERY

STELLA BIXBY

FERRY TAIL PUBLISHING LLC

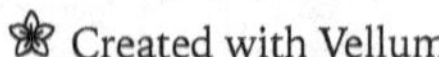 Created with Vellum

For my readers

ace irritated my shoulders, but his smile made the discomfort bearable. I'd do practically anything for the man in front of me. Including wearing a gown with lace.

"Do you, Garrett, take Rylie to be your lawfully wedded wife? To have and to hold from this day forward? For better or for worse? For richer or for poorer? In sickness and in health? As long as you both shall live?"

Garrett smiled his gorgeous smile and nodded. "I do."

I smiled back and tried to picture the life we'd have together.

I would officially move into his place. We'd have plenty of room for us, our two dogs, and our future children. Shayla—my best friend and roommate—would get our apartment all to herself. Well, she and her boyfriend, Seamus. I'd miss it, though. It was a really nice apartment. And Shayla was a fantastic roommate.

"Rylie?" The pastor Garrett's mom had chosen nodded at me with a sweet smile. He had to be at least a hundred years old, smelled like peppermint extract, and only came up to my shoulder.

And he was waiting for my response.

"Uh, yes," I said. "I absolutely do."

Garrett beamed.

"The word of God tells us what love is and what love does," the pastor continued. "Love is patient . . ."

Garrett had definitely been patient with me. Especially with all the murders I'd insisted on investigating.

"Love is kind."

Garrett was so kind. Sometimes too kind. Like the kind of kind that made you think he was hiding something. But he wasn't. That was just Garrett.

"Love is not jealous."

Eh. I mean, sometimes it was. Garrett was definitely jealous of my exes. I'd met none of Garrett's exes, so I had little to be jealous of.

Score one for me?

"Love does not brag and is not arrogant. It does not act unbecomingly. It does not seek its own, it is not easily provoked, and it does not hold grudges."

I could get behind all that. I smiled at Garett, and he smiled back. Were we really getting married?

I glanced down at the shoes pinching my heels. Nope, not a dream. That pain was real.

". . . for love bears all things, believes all things, hopes all things, and endures all things, but above all, love never fails."

Never fails.

The glimmer in Garrett's eyes said he would never fail me.

But what about me?

I swallowed.

I could do this.

Everyone said these things at their weddings, but no one was perfect.

I glanced back at my parents, who smiled at each other.

They said vows like this. But, surely, they'd failed one another a time or two? Right?

"Having this love in your hearts for one another, you have chosen to exchange rings as the sign and seal of the vows you are making to one another today."

Garrett and I turned our attention to the pastor.

"Garrett, will you please take this ring, place it on the third finger of Rylie's hand, and repeat after me: with this ring, I thee wed."

Garrett reached down and grabbed my left hand.

The pastor leaned in and whispered, "Of course, tomorrow, you will actually have a ring to do this with."

Garrett and I laughed as Garrett acted as if he were slipping a ring onto my finger and said, "With this ring, I thee wed."

The pastor nodded. "And Rylie, will you please take this ring, place it on the third finger of Garrett's hand, and repeat after me: with this ring, I thee wed."

I held Garrett's hand and did the same. "With this ring, I thee wed." I laughed a little at the charade.

"And at this point, I will pronounce you husband and wife and tell you, you can kiss your bride."

Garrett wrapped an arm around my waist and pulled

me into him, laying an incredibly passionate kiss on my lips.

One of the groomsmen groaned. Probably Scott, as he and I hadn't seemed to hit it off quite yet.

When we separated, a few people in the room clapped, and we walked back out like Zen had instructed us—the wedding planner for the Big Mountain Lodge and Resort.

Some of the wedding party couldn't make it to the rehearsal, so the procession was a bit skimpy, but they'd assured me they'd make it by the next morning.

Shayla had to work the late shift as a police officer. She and Seamus would drive down after her shift and bring our dogs—Fizzy and Babbitt—for the ceremony. Nikki—my other bridesmaid—would leave after her ranger shift at the reservoir and would be lucky to make it to the rehearsal dinner.

Garrett's groomsmen had all arrived in time. His family had late flights but would be here first thing tomorrow morning. My sister, her husband, and their four boys had driven up with my parents.

"It sounds like snow is coming," my mom said, picking a non-existent piece of lint off my lace dress. It wasn't my wedding dress—which also had lace by Garrett's request. It was a pale pink cocktail dress with a full skirt that reached just above my ankles.

"How much snow?" I asked. "Like a light dusting?"

She shook her head. "Like your senior year."

She and my dad had moved away from Big Mountain the minute I'd graduated. Something about better jobs in the city. Blah, blah, blah. I still didn't get it. Big Mountain was the most beautiful place in the entire world.

Heck, I probably would have lived here my entire life if it hadn't been for my ex cheating on me. He was in jail now, but that was a whole other story.

Either way, the snowstorm Mom was talking about was the single time we had a snow day in my entire kindergarten through twelfth-grade education. We'd gotten six feet of snow overnight. The busses literally could not get out of the bus barn. At least for a day. They got out before the second snow day.

"Let's just hope the news is wrong," Dad said, kissing me on top of my head. "It often is."

Mom shrugged.

If the news wasn't wrong, we'd easily be snowed in. Panic welled in my chest. We couldn't be snowed in. Our wedding would be ruined. All the money my parents had spent would be gone.

"It will be fine," Garrett said, squeezing my hand. "There's nothing we can't endure together, just like our vows said."

He was right. We would get through this together just like we had all the other crazy things we'd been through. Like the last time I'd involved myself in a murder investigation and had nearly gotten both of us killed.

I shook my head. I wouldn't think about that. After the wedding, I'd have some serious decisions to make, like whether I'd go back to work as a park ranger, but right now, I needed to be happy. To enjoy this once-in-a-lifetime event.

I forced a smile.

"Should we head over to get some drinks before the

rehearsal dinner?" Megan, my sister, said. "I think the groomsmen are getting antsy."

She motioned to the three men Garrett had chosen, who were now seeing how high they could throw a peanut in the air before catching it in their mouths. Cedric—Garrett's college roommate and an enormous black man—was winning.

"Speaking of the rehearsal dinner," Zen said, coming to stand next to me. He was so quiet, I barely knew when he was around, "what do you want to do about the extra plates?" He stood waiting for an answer—his hair perfectly groomed, his clothes pressed, and his fingernails exceptionally spotless. I suspected he used his full employee benefits package when it came to using the spa at a discount.

Mom stepped in. "I'll take this one."

Garrett corralled his groomsmen, and we all made our way to the massive room Blake—the hotel owner—had called the den when we did our walk-through of the resort. I'd visited the resort many times as a kid but never thought I'd get married here. It was so beautiful and grand—a place where rich people got married. Not the kid who grew up in town.

I'd never been in the den as a kid. I'd spent most of my time in the pool, where they let the local kids swim for a nominal fee.

"How's Garrett doing with the whole brother thing?" Megan whispered next to me as we walked.

Garrett's twin brother—Derrick—was in prison for murder. And kidnapping . . . me.

"I think he's okay," I said. "Or he's not thinking about it."

He and Cedric were now in a contest to get peanuts in their mouths while walking. I smiled. I couldn't wait to see Garrett in a tux.

"Ooh, watch out," I said too late as Garrett walked straight into a tiny woman. Thankfully, the man by her side held her hand, keeping her upright. Garrett, on the other hand, went down like a ton of bricks, trying not to take her with him.

I rushed to his side, but his gaze was locked on the woman helping him up—a tiny blonde with massive boobs.

"Eloise?" Garrett said.

Cedric whipped around to see, letting his peanut fall to the ground.

I stood back and tried to figure out what was going on.

"Garrett," Eloise said in a sweet voice. "It's so good to see you."

Garrett towered over her, but from his posture, it was obvious she held the power.

"Who is Eloise?" Megan mumbled to me.

I shrugged. "No idea."

Garrett was still holding the hand Eloise had used to help him up.

The man she had been holding hands with slipped an arm around her shoulder. "Why don't you introduce me to your friend, sweetheart." His voice was tense.

She looked at the man for a fraction of a second as if

she had no idea who he was before snapping out of her trance and dropping Garrett's hand.

"Nathan, this is Garrett," she said. "Garrett, this is Nathan. My fiancé."

Garrett's eyes widened, and his gaze flickered to Eloise's hand. Sure enough, there was a diamond on her third finger.

"It's very nice to meet you, Nathan," Garrett said. "I didn't know Eloise was engaged."

Nathan smiled and squeezed Eloise's shoulder. "We're very happy together."

Garrett looked stunned.

I rushed to his side. "Hi," I said, extending a hand to Eloise. "I'm Rylie, Garrett's fiancée."

Eloise didn't take my hand, but Nathan did. "We're pleased to meet you, aren't we, Eloise?"

Eloise looked up at him as if remembering she was, in fact, engaged. And not to Garrett.

"Eloise was my girlfriend in college," Garrett said, slipping an arm around my back and grabbing hold of my waist. "I proposed but—"

"I said no," Eloise said. "One of the biggest mistakes of my life."

Uh, okay. I glanced at Garrett, but he was still staring at Eloise.

"But if not for that, I would have never found Nathan," Eloise said, recovering. She turned and kissed Nathan with so much tongue it looked like two snakes making out.

"On that note, we have to go," Garrett said, interrupting their impromptu make-out session. "It was nice seeing you again."

"You as well," Eloise said. "And a pleasure to meet the woman with whom Garrett will spend the rest of his life."

I smiled. "Congratulations on your engagement, too. Are you getting married here at the resort?"

"We just came to see the place," Nathan said. "Our wedding is a couple of months away."

"And when is your wedding?" Eloise said.

Garrett squeezed me. "Tomorrow," he said with a smile that erased all of my worries. "We get married tomorrow."

"Ooh," Eloise said. "Let's hope this snowstorm holds off."

"I'm sure it will," Garrett said. "But even if it doesn't, everything will be okay." He was speaking to me now.

I smiled up at him. "Everything will be okay." I turned my focus back to Eloise. "Would the two of you like to join us for some drinks before our rehearsal dinner? We're just headed into the den."

Nathan started to say no, but Eloise interrupted. "We would love to."

2

Every time I was in the den, I felt like I had been transported into a fairytale. Huge windows from floor to vaulted-two-story ceiling showcased a hazy mountain view behind a steady snowfall. A stone fireplace added warmth and coziness. And the bar in the back corner made just about every drink imaginable.

"Rylie?" Selena, Cedric's wife, said when I was three drinks in. "Are you okay?"

"Do you think we're going to get snowed in?" I asked. "Because if we're snowed in, everyone else will be snowed out, and how will we have a wedding if everyone is snowed out? We'll have so much extra food and—"

"Deep breaths," Selena said. "It will be okay."

I took a couple of breaths, hating the verbal vomit coming from my mouth. "I'm sorry I'm being a bridezilla."

"Bridezilla?" Zen laughed behind me. "If you want to see a bridezilla, you only have to look over there."

He pointed to where Garrett, Cedric, and Eloise stood

reminiscing about their college days. Nathan and I had left the conversation after the first few minutes of being left out. It wasn't so much that I minded, but the way Eloise looked at Garrett made me uncomfortable. Especially with her fiancé standing right there.

"She doesn't look like a bridezilla," I said. "She looks practically perfect."

"She's the devil in human form," Zen said before rushing away to take care of something or other.

I glanced down at my pink dress and felt stupid. Eloise was in a form-fitting black slip dress with sky-high heels, and her hair pulled off her face.

"Cedric hates her," Selena said. She always seemed to pick up on other people's emotions.

"He doesn't look like he hates her," I said as they all laughed at probably another inside joke.

"He hates what she did to Garrett."

"What did she do to Garrett?" I sipped the magical tonic Blake had dubbed the Rylie when I liked it so much on our tour.

"Haven't you had your exes discussion?" Selena asked. "Most couples talk about these things before they get married."

I shrugged. "He never brought it up, so I figured it wasn't a big deal."

She laughed. "It's the ones they don't bring up that are the biggest deal."

"Do you think I should be worried?"

"Nah," she said with a nervous laugh. "I mean, you're both engaged now. I'm sure neither of them is thinking about what could have been."

Except they were. Or at least, Eloise was. She mentioned before that saying no to his proposal was the worst decision she'd ever made.

I sighed. *Love is not jealous.* That was supposed to be my advantage—I wasn't the jealous one. And here I was ruining that too. How could I stand in front of everyone and make all those vows when I knew I'd end up ruining them all?

"Rylie?" Selena said. "Get out of your head. Let's talk about something else."

I shook my head from side to side, trying to dislodge the doubts trying to derail everything. "How's the little guy?"

Selena was the little boy's stepmother, but she'd raised him since he was born.

"He's good," she said. "He's upstairs with the nanny. I couldn't imagine leaving him at home."

"Do you think you and Cedric will have any more kids?" I asked.

"Who knows," she said. "What about you? Are you going to start your family sooner or later?"

"Garrett would say sooner."

"And you?"

I shrugged. "Things have been so crazy with everything I haven't really thought about it."

That was a total lie, and Selena knew it. I'd been sitting around in a fog since I'd tried—unsuccessfully—to quit my job. I'd had nothing but time to think about it. And the more I thought about it, the more I worried. Would I be a good mom? Did I need to have kids so soon?

"Don't think about it too hard," she said, taking my

hand. "I never thought I wanted to be a mom until it was practically thrown in my lap. Now, I love it. And I know you will too. I've seen you with those nephews of yours. They adore you. You're great with them."

"I know I want kids . . . eventually."

I felt two strong hands on my shoulders, and a kiss pressed into my hair. "I'm sorry about that," Garrett said behind me. "I didn't expect to see Eloise here."

He and Cedric took their places next to Selena and me.

"It's okay," I said with a smile I hoped looked real. "I'm the one who invited them in for drinks."

"It's been such a long time," Garrett said.

"And she hasn't changed a bit," Cedric said, a warning in his tone.

"Dude," Garrett said. "I'm happily engaged. And tomorrow, I marry the woman of my dreams."

I smiled for real this time. "We should probably get to the rehearsal dinner, don't you think?"

Garrett looked at his watch. "I'm sorry, babe. I didn't realize it was so late. I would never have spent so much time talking to—"

"You're fine," I said. "But we better go before my mom has a conniption and walks all the way down here to gather us herself."

We walked hand-in-hand down the hallway after gathering everyone associated with the wedding. Eloise and Nathan seemed to have disappeared, which was probably for the best. If Luke had been able to make it—even though he and I were a thing of the past and he was literally in the Middle East—Garrett wouldn't have felt terribly comfortable either.

Even the hallways of the resort were beautiful. Artwork that hadn't been there when I was a kid graced the halls. "Can you believe we're getting married here?" Excitement welled in my chest.

Garrett spun me around and picked me up in his hulking arms. "I am so excited."

He kissed me gently.

"Get a room," Cedric said with a laugh.

"It's too bad we can't spend tonight together," Garrett said.

"It might be a silly tradition, but it's still a tradition," I said. "I wouldn't want to jinx us before we've even started."

He kissed me again. "But how will I stay warm?"

I laughed, and he put me back on the ground. "Maybe that's why they say we should stay away from each other the night before the wedding, so we can remember how horrible it was sleeping alone."

"I'm pretty sure the tradition came from when men and women didn't sleep together until they were married," Selena said. "Now, fix your skirt, and let's go."

I smoothed down the front of my dress as we walked into a small but cozy dining room.

"There you are," Mom said. "The food is getting cold."

I took my place at the head table. "Sorry, we got sidetracked."

"I ran into an old friend," Garrett said. "Small world."

"Small world?" Scott said. "She hunted you down. The

only reason she's considering getting married here is because she found out you are."

"How do you know?" Garrett asked.

"Her sister is friends with my sister," Scott said. "They were talking about it the other day."

"Is her sister hot too?" Hugo, the other groomsman, asked.

"I got dibs," Scott said. "Plus, we already had a thing. She should be here soon to check out the resort with Eloise. I'd watch your six. I think Eloise is here for more than just planning her wedding."

Hugo laughed. "She didn't want you until she found out you had someone else? That's messed up."

Garrett squeezed my hand. "She seemed pretty smitten with Nathan. Plus, I made it perfectly clear how much I love Rylie."

Cedric laughed. "And did you see her face when you did? She looked like she'd eaten hot coals."

The other guys laughed too.

I was only too thankful when Megan sat down next to us and changed the topic of conversation. "Kids are freaking crazy." She tucked a stray piece of hair behind her ear. "The boys were playing hide and seek in the hotel room, and Tom fell asleep. When he woke up, they couldn't find Devin. The older boys got bored trying to find him and started playing video games. When we finally found him in the air return, he was fast asleep."

"He crawled into the air return?" I asked.

She shrugged. "There are only so many places to hide in a hotel room."

I laughed. If I ever did have kids, I'd be calling Megan

every other day for advice. Alex, Bryce, Chase, and Devin —her boys, named alphabetically—were challenging on an easy day. Her stamina with them amazed me.

A soft clinking came from the table in front of us. Dad stood.

"You know, I never thought we'd be back in Big Mountain to celebrate Rylie's wedding." He seemed a bit choked up. "Sure, she talked about getting married in the mountains, but we always had her pegged for the one who would elope."

"She tried," Garrett said.

"I did not." I laughed.

"Kidding," Garrett said.

"Either way," Dad continued. "I'm so happy to have everyone here who could make it. I pray tomorrow is the day Rylie has dreamed about since the moment she *finally* said yes to Garrett's proposal."

Everyone in the room laughed.

"Here's to the couple." Dad raised his glass. "May they encourage each other each day to be their best selves and never let one another settle for mediocrity."

"Here here," the group said, toasting and drinking the delicious champagne I didn't even want to see the bill for.

My parents had refused to let Garrett pay for anything but the rehearsal dinner, and it showed. Garrett had gone all out creating a menu that included food from all over the world. I'd tried to convince him to use that money for the honeymoon, but he assured me he had plenty set aside for our mystery trip.

I'd never heard of a groom surprising his bride with a mystery honeymoon, but Garrett had been adamant. He'd seen it on a TV show when he was a kid and had always thought about what he'd do.

Shayla assured me I'd be happy with it, so I went along. I told him as long as the weather was warm and there were activities to do, I'd be happy.

The wait staff was incredibly friendly and, about halfway through the meal, Blake arrived.

Zen nearly fell backward over a chair when he saw her. "I didn't think you were coming in tonight."

"I wanted to make sure everything was on track," she said to Zen, then looked at me. "How has everything been thus far?"

"It's been lovely," I said. "Is everything okay?"

I didn't know whether it was the way she was standing or the tone of her voice, but I could tell something was up.

"As you know, my mother is the chief of police."

I closed my eyes and took a breath. She couldn't possibly be telling me someone died. I did not need a murder the night before my wedding.

When I opened my eyes, she continued. "She notified me that if the storm continues, the roads will be closed."

It was better than a dead body but still sucked. "If they're closed, when will they reopen?"

"It's hard to say," Blake said.

"Then we just need to hope they don't close," Garrett said.

Blake nodded. "But we should be prepared for the worst."

I took a breath. "Which means?"

"That's up to you," she said. "We could go forward

with the wedding and the people here. Many of the staff will go home shortly and may not make it back, including the hairstylists and chefs. Of course, we have a staff that remains on site at times like these. We won't leave you without the necessities. And I, myself, will stay to help accommodate any requests you may have. However, I do not know how long this storm is supposed to last. Several of the staff members have families they need to attend to."

"I completely understand," I said. "I'm okay with them leaving."

"I'm not," Garrett said. "Rylie deserves the wedding she wants."

"And she can have it," Blake continued. "That's the other option. As soon as the storm subsides, we can go forward as planned. We don't have another wedding scheduled until next weekend, and the storm is supposed to die down within the next couple of days. We will arrange for the wedding to proceed at no extra cost to you. We will also not charge you for the extra nights you would be staying." Blake took a breath. "However, you are welcome to get married tomorrow. The wedding may be a bit more modest than what you planned, but I understand if the date has importance to you."

"The date is not of importance," I said. "But can we play it by ear? I'd like to hold out hope that perhaps the weather will take a turn away from us, and the roads will reopen in the morning."

"Absolutely," Blake said, handing me a business card. "And please, call my cell with any requests you have. If the staff isn't around, I will do it myself. Including your hair, if you choose to stay tomorrow. I've been known for my amazing up-dos."

I smiled. "Thank you."

When she walked away, Garrett slumped back in his chair. "I'm sorry, Rylie. I know this isn't what you had planned."

"I'm okay," I said. "If tomorrow doesn't work, I can easily wait for the next day or the next. What's a couple of extra days in the grand scheme of things?" I stopped. "Except, what about the honeymoon? Are we going to miss flights or anything?"

Garrett waved a hand. "Don't you even worry about it." Then he smiled. "I'm not giving up information that easily."

I thought I had him for a second. "I love you."

"I love you too."

3

Garrett and I explained everything to my mom and dad, then to the rest of the bridal party.

"It sounds good to me," Tom, my brother-in-law, said. "I bet the boys will love having the run of this place. There are probably some epic hiding places."

"No," Megan said. "No way. You already lost one of them in our four hundred square foot room. There's absolutely no way I'm letting my baby roam an entire lodge."

Tom shrugged. "Let's make the most of it. It's not every day you get snowed into an awesome lodge in the middle of the Colorado Rockies."

As cool as that sounded, I hoped the snow would keep moving and let us have the wedding we planned for tomorrow.

"Does that mean we can stay in the same room tonight?" Garrett asked, his hand making its way up my leg.

I giggled. "No," I said. "Because then we for sure can't

have the wedding tomorrow. Even if everything works out."

"What if it doesn't?" he asked. "Will you still want to try to make it happen tomorrow?"

"I don't know," I said. "What do you think?"

"Your parents paid good money for the wedding you wanted. If we just go forward with it tomorrow, their money will be wasted." He smiled. "I think we hold out until it's perfect."

I nodded. "I'll let Blake know she won't have to practice her famous up-do on me."

I was reaching for my phone when I heard someone shouting outside the dining room. "What's that?"

Garrett stood and moved toward the door. I followed. The rest of the room hushed.

"I cannot believe you were flirting with him," a man's voice shouted.

It sounded like a woman was crying. "I wasn't flirting. He's just a friend."

"Oh, sure," the man said. "A friend you used to sleep with."

"We were going to get married," the woman said. "We were in love."

"If you want to marry him, marry him."

"I can't. He's engaged. And so am I," she added quickly. "I'm happy with you. I love you."

"You didn't show it when you were all giggly with Mr. Bodybuilder. What is that guy, some sort of superhero in disguise?"

I looked up at Garrett, who blushed. Then the entire

thing came into perspective. The man and woman outside were Nathan and Eloise.

"I didn't mean to make you feel bad," Eloise said.

"Feel bad?" The man laughed. "You made me feel terrible. Like I wasn't worth your time. Just go. Go in there and tell him how you feel. That's what you wanted to do, right? That's why you're stalking outside their rehearsal dinner?"

I glanced up at Garrett again, whose face flushed with anger.

"I wasn't stalking outside," she said. "I didn't even know this was the room until I walked by. I was just trying to clear my head."

"Then come back to the room."

"No," she said. "I don't want to."

"You'll come back with me or else—"

Garrett had had enough. He threw open the door and shouted, "Or else what?"

Nathan didn't look even the slightest bit surprised. "This doesn't concern you."

"If she doesn't want to go with you, she doesn't have to," Garrett said, his tone threatening.

Eloise rushed to Garrett's side—the side opposite me—and grabbed onto his arm.

"Are you okay?" I peeked around Garret and asked her, but she didn't take her eyes off Garrett.

Garrett, however, was still focused on Nathan.

"I wasn't going to do anything," Nathan said, holding his hands up in surrender. "Isn't that right, E? It's not like I'm abusive."

She shrugged. "No, you're not."

"I just want you to come with me," Nathan said. "I am your fiancé after all."

She dropped her arms to her sides and moved away from Garrett. "I'm sorry, sugar." She kissed him again with the snake-kiss.

Garrett ran a hand through his hair. "Maybe we should get back to our dinner."

He turned, and I followed him back inside, where everyone stood staring at us.

When I looked back, Eloise's perfect heart-shaped face drooped, and she and Nathan walked away hand-in-hand. I don't know what she was hoping would happen, but maybe she needed someone to remind her that Garrett was taken.

"That was awfully convenient," Megan said when I sat down next to her.

"What do you mean?" I glanced over at Garrett, who was leaning over, talking to Cedric and Scott.

"She just happens to get into a huge argument with her fiancé right outside your rehearsal dinner door?" Megan said. "We need to keep an eye on her. She's plotting."

"It doesn't matter," I said. "Garrett's a good guy. He won't ruin what we have for someone who turned him down years ago."

"Are you certain Garrett doesn't still have a thing for her?"

"It's probably a lot like Luke and me. She was his first love, so he feels connected to her somehow. But, unlike Luke and me, I don't think Eloise has gotten over Garrett."

"I'd say that's pretty clear."

I took a huge drink of my Rylie cocktail. "Her fiancé seems to be the jealous type."

"Do you think he's dangerous?"

That was the last thing we needed—a dangerous, jealous man trapped inside a hotel with us. "I hope not. Eloise said he wasn't."

Megan didn't look convinced. "I'll keep an eye on both of them."

I smiled. She was the best big sister a girl could hope for.

"I am so sorry," Zen said, appearing at my side. "I don't know how she snuck away and ended up outside your dining room."

"It's okay," I said. "She's harmless."

"Is she, though?" Zen said. "She's screamed at nearly the entire staff, broken her fair share of stemmed glasses because they had smudges, and tried to get me fired."

"She tried to get you fired?" I asked.

"She said I was hitting on her," Zen said. "It's a good thing Blake knows I am in no way attracted to women, regardless of the size of their ta-tas."

I laughed. "But you're still working with her?"

"I have to prove to Blake I can be the event planner she needs me to be. Which means dealing with hard-to-work-with brides." He kissed my hand. "I'm just thankful you've been nothing but a sweetheart."

I sighed. "What did Garrett ever see in her? How could he have been attracted to both of us?"

"Men's brains don't mature as early as women's,"

Megan said. "He probably saw a nice rack, and his hormones did the rest. With you, it's real love."

I didn't know whether to be happy about that or not. I mean, I knew I didn't have big boobs, but I still wanted his hormones to be attracted to me.

I took a bite of the food in front of me but realized I wasn't hungry anymore.

I also realized Garrett had disappeared from the table.

"Do you know where Garrett went?" I asked Cedric.

He glanced up from his plate and looked around. "Probably to the bathroom or something."

I stood, but Megan grabbed my arm. "You don't think he went off to look for that girl, do you?"

I shook my head. "Cedric's probably right. Garrett's probably in the bathroom. I was just going to use the bathroom myself. You know, the power of suggestion and all."

Megan didn't even pretend she believed me, but she let go of my arm.

I snuck out the side door behind the bridal party table so my mother wouldn't make a big fuss about me leaving. If she noticed both Garrett and I were gone, she'd probably freak out. But I wouldn't be gone long. And I could go to the bathroom if I wanted to. I was a big girl.

The bathrooms were down the hall to the right. Instead, I went left—the direction Eloise and Nathan had gone. I figured that would be the way Garrett went, too . . . if he was following her. Which he probably wasn't.

I changed my mind and turned back toward the bathrooms. *Love is not jealous.* Garrett had given me no reason not to trust him. I needed to get over this stupid little jealousy.

We were getting married in the morning, after all.

When I was securely inside a stall, I heard the door open.

"I don't think it's going to happen," Blake said, probably into her phone. "The roads are nearly impassable. The entire wedding party is going to be stuck on the other side of the pass."

She had to be talking about my wedding. I choked back the emotion that threatened to pour out onto my cheeks.

"I feel so bad for her." Blake paused. "That bridezilla I've been dealing with is her fiancé's ex-girlfriend. It's bad enough to stay in the same vicinity as that woman without her hitting on your fiancé the day before your canceled wedding."

"Whose wedding is canceled?" Another voice asked.

"I gotta go. Kiss the kids for me when you tuck them in," Blake said. "Eloise, how lovely to see you."

"Whose wedding is canceled?" Eloise asked again. "Did Garrett call it off? I mean, I knew we'd still have a spark, but *wow*. That didn't take long at all."

Every bit of me wanted to bust down the stall door and wring her tiny little neck. Instead, I stayed as still as possible to hear how Blake would reply.

"Did I say canceled?" Blake asked. "I meant postponed. Garrett dearly loves Rylie. Just as Nathan dearly loves you."

"Right," Eloise said. "Nathan loves me. Of course, he does. What's not to love? It's only natural for men to fawn over me. Anyway, it's not like I want them to cancel their wedding. I just thought since Garrett acted so protective of me, that it was a possibility."

"Garrett seems like a man who would protect just about anyone in trouble," Blake said.

If I could have given her a high-five, I would have.

"Hopefully, Kylie isn't the jealous type," Eloise said.

"Rylie," Blake corrected. "And I don't think she is."

Eloise giggled. "Thank you so much for being so hospitable. I promise we won't get in the way this week-end. I'm hoping this will be the right venue for our *very expensive* wedding."

"Remind me, how did you hear about us?" Blake asked.

"Oh, uh, well, I—" Eloise cleared her throat, then lowered her voice to a whisper. "I may have gotten wind that this is where Garrett was getting married. And I figured if it was good enough for him, it was good enough for me."

Blake was quiet for a moment, then said, "Rylie and Garrett are paying customers, as you may one day become. This means it's my job to protect them, just as it would be my job to protect you if you were to have your wedding here. Therefore, I'm urging you to stay away from Garrett. Sometimes it's hard to give up on our exes, but you have an amazing man in Nathan."

Eloise giggled again, though this time, it sounded a bit more forced. "I'm sure Kylie doesn't need any protecting. She's a big-time park ranger, you know. Catching bad guys and stuff."

"Rylie," Blake corrected again, "is plenty capable of holding down her man."

"Then why do you seem so worried?" Eloise asked.

Blake didn't reply.

When the door opened and closed, I waited a bit to make sure they were both gone. After a few minutes of silence, I walked out to find Blake with her hands on her hips, staring at me.

"How long did you know I was in there?" I asked.

"I only realized after she pranced out of here like a poodle with a new hairdo." Blake sighed. "I'm sorry you had to hear that. You have nothing to worry about with Garrett and Eloise."

"I'm not worried," I said. "At least not about him. Her, on the other hand . . ."

"She's harmless," Blake said. "Did you decide what you wanted to do?"

"I think we'll postpone the wedding if the roads end up closing," I said. "No use stressing everyone out when we can easily get married in a couple of days."

"That makes perfect sense. And I'll be here to make sure your accommodations are perfect in the meantime."

"Don't you have kids?" I asked.

Blake nodded.

"Go home to them," I said. "As long as there's food, water, and heat, we'll be fine here. Heck, I'd even be okay fixing my own food if you don't think the health department would be upset."

Blake laughed. "I'm most definitely not allowing you to make your own food. We have a barebones staff that lives here for times exactly like these."

"Perfect," I said. "Then until the wedding is a go— whether that's tomorrow or a few days from now—you should go home and be with your family. Snowstorms are the perfect times to create memories. I remember getting snowed in with my family. We'd play board games, do puzzles, read books, make cocoa. It was wonderful."

"We have all of those things in the den," Blake said.

"Now, you're talking," I said. "Tomorrow, I may or may not be getting married, but either way, my day won't be ruined. Give me hot cocoa and a board game, and I'm good to go."

"You're certain you don't need me here?" Blake seemed torn.

"Absolutely," I said. "A few days of being snowed-in won't hurt anything."

4

———

I left the bathroom and headed back toward the dining room, but voices echoed from the opposite direction.

I tip-toed down the hallway toward the voices. Spying wasn't something I often did, but one of the voices sounded like Garrett's, and the other sounded like Eloise's.

Everything in me hoped it wasn't them. That I was wrong. Or, if I wasn't, that it was just a loud conversation between two old friends.

But as I neared the turn in the hallway, I could tell it wasn't just loud. It was emotion-filled.

"I don't understand why you're even with her," Eloise said.

"Because I love her," Garrett said.

"I can tell there's a part of you that still loves me too."

I waited for a reply that didn't come.

"It's okay. You can say it." Eloise's voice was almost seductive.

"No," Garrett said. "I can't. We had our chance. Now, it's Rylie's turn."

My turn? Yuck.

"Didn't *Kylie* almost get you killed?"

"That wasn't completely her fault."

"I've seen the YouTube videos. Attention seeker much? Or is she just trying to get herself into trouble?"

Videos? There were multiple videos? I made a mental note to search for said videos.

"She's big on helping people," Garrett said. "Sure, it's scary, but I think she's tiring of being a park ranger, anyway. This last case really shook her up."

Everything he said was true, but the way he said it made me almost want to refute his statement.

"I like to help people too," Eloise said. "But I do it in a way that doesn't put anyone in danger."

"You help people with your daddy's money," Garrett said.

"What's the harm in that?"

Garrett sighed. "I suppose there's no harm in that. But I'm telling you right now, I am marrying Rylie. I made a promise, and I'm not one to back out on my promises."

Did he want to back out?

"I have to go," Garrett said. "I'm supposed to be at my rehearsal di—"

Everything went silent. I peeked around the corner to see them lip-locked.

"What the hell was that?" Garrett said, taking a step backward.

"Come on," Eloise said. "You know you've wanted to kiss me since the moment you saw me."

"I have to go."

Garrett came around the corner and nearly smacked right into me.

"Oh hi," he said, glancing behind him.

I plastered a smile on my face. "I was looking for you."

He wrapped an arm around my shoulder and led me down the hallway toward the dining room. "Eloise held me up."

We passed by an open closet door. Peeking out was a furious-looking Nathan.

I almost said something, but Blake walked out of the bathroom at that very moment.

"Oh look, there's the happy couple now," she said. "I was just thinking about how wonderful your wedding will be once this snow clears. We can even do pictures up on the roof if you want. The mountains will be stunning in the background."

I did my best to smile. Garrett squeezed me closer to him. "I can't wait."

"Me neither," I said. "It will be wonderful."

"And you're certain you're okay if I go home?" Blake asked.

Garrett gave me a questioning look. It was at that moment I noticed the lipstick on his lips.

"Yep," I said, turning my attention back to Blake. "Enjoy the time with your family. We'll be fine here until the snow lets up."

"Sounds good," she said. "Just call me on my cell if you need anything while I'm away. We have snowmobiles, snowshoes, and snow tires. I'll make it here if you need me."

"I'm sure that won't be necessary," Garrett said. "Thank you."

She walked back the way we'd just come from. I glanced back to see if she noticed Nathan in the closet, but the door was closed as Blake walked by. As frustrated as I was with Eloise, I didn't want Nathan to do anything stupid. If he'd heard or seen any of the exchange between Garrett and Eloise, I could understand his anger.

Heck, I was angry too.

"Did you kiss Eloise?" I asked, pulling away from Garrett.

"No," Garrett said, his hand reflexively wiping his lips. "I mean, yes. I mean, no. I didn't kiss her. But yes, we kissed. She kissed me. I pulled away. How long had you been there?"

"Long enough." I couldn't help the tears welling up in my eyes.

"I'm so sorry," Garrett said. "I should never have been down there with her in the first place."

"She is trying to get between us." The whininess in my voice made me cringe. I cleared my throat and managed a more normal voice. "I heard her in the bathroom talking to Blake about how you should be with her instead of me."

"She won't get between us. If almost getting murdered didn't push us apart, an old girlfriend won't."

The fact that I'd almost gotten Garrett killed had been brought up twice in a matter of minutes. He and I hadn't really talked about it since it happened. We'd both been avoiding it.

"Do you think I should quit being a park ranger?" I asked.

"I thought you already made that decision."

"What if I'm rethinking it?"

Garrett sighed. "You know I don't like you being in danger every waking moment. But if that's what you want to do, I won't stop you."

"Will that get between us?"

"No," he said. "Unless it really does get me killed."

I gaped at him.

"I'm kidding, babe." He laughed. "Can I hug you? I can't say I'm sorry enough for what happened with Eloise. I promise I'll stay far away from her the rest of my time here."

I opened my arms, and he squeezed me tight.

"Do you forgive me?" he asked.

"Yeah," I said. "It's not your fault she kissed you."

He let me go, and we walked back to the rehearsal dinner together.

"Where have the two of you been?" my mom asked. "You better not be doing the dirty the night before your wedding."

Garrett turned bright red. I wanted to ask her what she thought we did when I stayed at his house or he stayed at my apartment but didn't think it wise.

"On the subject of the wedding," I said, bringing my voice to an almost-shout. "Can everyone listen up for a moment?"

The room quieted. All eyes were on me.

"If the storm comes in like they expect it will tonight, the roads will be closed. In that instance, Garrett and I have decided we will postpone the wedding until the storm clears and the rest of the guests and wedding party can get here." I took a breath. "We're hoping that would be sometime this week. I understand this might be difficult for some of you who need to be back home or at work in the next few days. If you need to and can find a way out of here, I'd suggest you do so as soon as possible. You can always come back on the day of the wedding if you'd like. Otherwise, the hotel has agreed to let us stay for no additional fee until the wedding can take place. There will be food and beverages and maybe even a board game or two."

A couple of groans came from the groomsmen, but Garrett squeezed my hand in solidarity.

When no one made any move to leave, Garrett and I sat back down to finish our dinner before heading to the den for a round of charades.

On our way out of the dining room, as we passed the large double doors of the hotel entrance, the sound of a snowmobile came from the other side of the doors.

Everyone stopped to listen.

"What is that?" Megan asked.

We waited until the sound seemed to disappear. It was probably someone coming to check on the hotel. Or maybe it was Blake's ride home.

"It's charades time," I said, turning toward the den.

But the booming of the doors opening and the wind whipping the snow into the lobby stopped me in my tracks.

Standing in the doorway was a tiny snow-covered silhouette. "Are you just going to stand there, or are you going to help an old woman out?"

Garrett and his groomsmen hurried to the door. Two of them closed the doors against the storm while the other two helped the woman get out of her snowy clothes.

"Bernadette?" Garrett asked when he saw the woman's face.

"How's my ex-possible-son-in-law?" Her voice boomed through the lobby as she wrapped her arms around Garrett in a tight hug.

He patted her on the back. When I looked closer, it was apparent she was Eloise's mother. They had the same hair, nose, and plastic surgeon, by the looks of things.

Ugh.

Not only would I have to deal with a jealous ex-girlfriend, but her mother, too?

"Have you seen my daughter?" Bernadette asked as they walked toward the rest of us.

"Not recently," Garrett said, shooting me a guilty glance. "I would guess she's in her room with her fiancé."

"Nathan, yuck." Bernadette stuck her tongue out and spat like a baby trying mashed peas for the first time. "Fiancé might give him too much credit."

"They're here looking for a wedding venue," Garrett said. "And that rock on her hand seems to mean business."

"Everything Nathan does is a business proposition. Including marrying my daughter." Bernadette laced her arm through Garrett's and batted her eyelashes up at him. "Why couldn't she have said yes to you? You were so sweet and charming and perfect for her."

Garrett smiled, then caught himself and frowned. "Let me introduce you to my fiancée."

She turned her gaze to me. "Fiancée? Is that right?"

"It's nice to meet you," I said, trying to be the bigger person. I was getting tired, and my inner bridezilla was begging to come out.

"She's so . . ." She looked me up and down. "Plain."

"I'm sorry, who are you to call my daughter plain?" My mom stepped between Bernadette and me.

"Bernadette Livingston. I'm Eloise's mother." Bernadette turned to Garrett. "Looks like you could have done better on the mother-in-law front, too. What's gotten into you?"

"Stop," I said, unable to control myself. "First, your daughter kisses my fiancé. Then you have the nerve to show up on my wedding weekend and insult my mother and me?"

"Oh, sweetie," Bernadette said, her voice condescending. "Do you own this resort?"

"I—huh?"

"Because I have a reservation—paid in full—which gives me every right to be here." She looked at Garrett. "It's not Eloise's fault she's following her heart."

That was it. I wasn't in the mood for charades anymore. "I'm going to my room. Goodnight, everyone."

Megan followed me to the elevators.

When I looked back at the lobby, Garrett was standing in between my mom and Bernadette, looking like he'd bitten off more than he could chew. I almost felt bad for him. But he hadn't exactly run after me either. Not that I was walking away to have him run after me. I wasn't a teenager.

"Wanna talk about it?" Megan asked when the elevator doors closed.

"Eloise kissed Garrett."

"Yeah, I heard."

"And when she was talking to him about his relationship with me, he wasn't exactly standing up for it."

"Do you think he wants to be with her?" Megan asked.

"I'm not sure," I said. "He made it sound like the only reason he was marrying me was because he promised. I mean, I know he loves me. But what if he loves her more?"

"Do you love Luke more than Garrett?" Megan asked.

"No. Why would you even ask me that?"

Megan shrugged.

"Can we please stop talking about Luke? He's not here causing problems, is he?"

"No," Megan said. "Do you wish he were?"

"No," I blurted out. "I just want to get married. I want to walk down the aisle and say the words and get on with my new life."

"Do you, though?"

"Megan, stop." I stepped out of the elevator and headed toward my room. I needed to climb into bed and forget the world for a bit.

"I'm being serious," Megan said, coming after me. "Because if Tom kissed another woman, I'd be livid. I'd be freaking the hell out. And here you are just pushing it under the rug like it's no big deal."

"Maybe it's not a big deal," I said. "If she kissed him, and he pushed her away, why would I make a big deal about that?"

"What about what he said? Or, rather, didn't say?"

"You know what? I shouldn't have told you anything. I told you all the bad things about Troy and made you hate him. I don't want to do the same thing with Garrett."

"Troy was a douche canoe," Megan said. "That tried to freaking kill you."

"Well, Garrett's not. In fact, I'm the one who almost got him killed." I slid the card into the reader on the door. "I'm going to bed. I'll see you tomorrow. Try not to lose any of my nephews."

She smiled. "Don't be so hard on yourself about your last case. It wasn't your fault that lunatic drugged Garrett."

"Maybe not directly," I said. "But indirectly, it was. And I have to live with that."

"I love you, Sis."

"Love you too," I said and closed the door.

My bed was fluffy and inviting. I'd just taken off my lace dress and hung it in the closet when my peace was disturbed.

"Rylie? Can I come in?" Garrett's voice came from outside my door.

I stood and cracked the door open.

"I feel like a broken record, but I'm really sorry. Bernadette should never have come here. I don't know what she and Eloise are playing at, but it won't work."

"Do you want to be with her? Like, if you and I had never met, and you saw her again, would you want to be with her?"

"You know I can't assume what I would or wouldn't want in a different world. That's not logical."

"Say I called off the wedding right now? Gave you back your ring? Would you end up with Eloise?"

"Again," he said slowly. "I can't assume. Unless that's what you're doing."

My heart sped. "No." I shook my head. "That's not what I'm doing. Unless that's what you want me to do?"

"I think you're tired and stressed and maybe have a bit of cold feet." Garrett smiled. "Which is okay. I expected it from my wild and crazy girl."

"We make quite the couple, don't we?" I opened the door wider and let him in. "You, the solid, down-to-earth accountant. And me the—"

"Gorgeous park ranger." He looked me up and down as I stood in front of him in my bra and underwear. "Wow." Garrett took my face in his hands and kissed me.

When we stopped kissing, I said, "I'm sorry I put your life in danger."

"I have to stop wording it like that," Garrett said. "You didn't put my life in danger. Sure, what you do with the cases can be dangerous, but the fact that I was in danger was because some crazy person was trying to get away with murder."

"I just feel so bad," I said. "But I'll try to stop thinking about it."

"What about the job?" Garrett asked, sitting next to me on the bed.

"I'm not sure," I said. "I'm so tired. My brain can't handle any more contemplation."

"How about I tuck you in?" Garrett said.

"You're not going to stay?" I asked, getting under the covers.

"I think you're right about staying separately," he said. "It'll make our wedding night that much better. And we need to stay away from any more bad luck if we can."

Exhaustion took precedence over arguing. "Our wedding night will be amazing."

"I count on it," Garrett said, kissing me so passionately I almost pulled him into bed. "I'll see you in the morning."

"Goodnight," I said as he walked to the door and turned off the lights.

5

I t was too bad my brain couldn't get on board with my body's need for sleep. Or maybe it was my body that wouldn't let my brain sleep.

Either way, I wasn't sleeping.

I slipped out from beneath the soft sheets and fluffy duvet and changed into my swimming suit. I pulled on a robe and some flip-flops and headed down to the hot tub.

The hotel was silent. When we were kids, we used to talk about how the resort was haunted, but we'd never actually encountered proof of that fact.

The smell of chlorine and cleaning solution hit my nose and took me back to my childhood. I inhaled and closed my eyes, allowing it to calm me. This was my wedding weekend. I deserved peace and joy.

The water in the hot tub was completely still, with steam rising from the surface to the ceiling, where it collected into condensation and dripped down the wall. I took off my robe and flip-flops, leaving them on a nearby chair before dipping a toe, then an ankle, and finally my whole body to my chin in the all-encompassing warmth.

When I closed my eyes, I could almost hear the giggles echoing from when I was a teenager, jumping and splashing into the pool with my friends . . . and Luke. We used to make the older people so angry when we splashed them in the hot tub with the cold pool water.

I dipped my head back, so the only thing still above water was my mouth, nose, and eyes, and let my body float to the surface.

I imagined the sound of footsteps, the drip of cold water splashing across my face.

Except, it wasn't my imagination.

I opened my eyes to see two enormous hands reaching for my face.

Instinctively, I took a deep breath before the hands pushed my entire head underwater.

I struggled to get my feet under me, but once I did, I pushed up hard, coming to a stand.

Scott knelt by the side of the hot tub, doubled over in laughter.

I splashed hot water at him and moved to sit on the opposite side of the tub.

"You look—" He gasped for air. "Like—you look—" His boisterous laugh echoed off the walls. Any bit of calm I might have had was gone in an instant.

"Come off it," I said, wrapping my arms around my chest. "What the hell were you doing?"

"Just a joke," he managed, then slid into the hot tub opposite me. He wiped the tears from his eyes and finally stopped laughing. "Did you think I was going to drown you?"

"Something like that," I admitted, trying to laugh it off.

"I couldn't resist," he said. "You looked so chill. You're lucky I didn't do a cannonball into the tub."

I searched for any hint of maliciousness behind his eyes. Had he just been messing around, or were there more sinister motives behind him holding my head underwater?

I took a deep breath and let it out. He was Garrett's friend. Of course, he wasn't trying to kill me. Why would he do that?

A little voice in the back of my head said—*because he hates you.*

"So? Why are you down here?" Scott asked.

"Just trying to relax."

"Ah." Scott laughed. "Guess I ruined that for you." He was the furthest thing from apologetic.

My temper flared. "Why are *you* down here?" It was then I noticed he was wearing jeans. "You're not even wearing swimming trunks."

He laughed again. It took everything in me not to dip his head beneath the water. "Just needed to warm up."

"Warm up?" I asked. "Why?"

"Got stuck outside without a shirt on," he said as if it was the most normal thing in the world to get trapped outside in the middle of the night in a snowstorm. "No shoes either."

He lifted a foot out of the water and showed me a sock with a hole that let his big toe pop out.

Every bit of me wanted to exit the hot tub and make a run for my hotel room. But I couldn't let him see any more weakness, or he'd keep teasing me mercilessly. Plus, I hadn't thought to grab a towel, and Scott was now directly between my robe and me.

"How exactly does one get stuck outside without a shirt on?" I asked, trying to keep my tone light.

"It's a long story," he said. "Hugo and I were seeing who could take the most shots and then—"

What sounded like a scream interrupted his story.

I jumped out of the hot tub as quickly as I could and started running toward the scream.

My mother's warnings from my childhood echoed in my head as my foot slipped on the smooth concrete. *Running by the pool makes you a fool. You'll fall with a thud and lose all your blood.*

I did my best not to let my head hit the concrete, but my back and tailbone weren't as lucky.

"Damn," Scott said from the hot tub. "That looked like it hurt."

The scream penetrated the air again.

I tried to get to my feet. As much as it hurt to fall, someone else sounded like they were in real trouble.

"Chill, girl. It's just my alarm." He reached out of the water to grab his phone, obviously not worried about it getting wet as he started tapping the screen. "Gotta go. Do you need help up?"

I shook my head. "I'm fine." The last thing I wanted was him touching me.

"Sorry about ruining your relaxation time. You really

seem to need it." He walked toward the men's locker room. "Oh, and nice bikini."

His words made me feel dirty. Why was he commenting on my bikini? It wasn't like I wanted him ogling me. Gross.

My back was already stiff as I tried to peel myself off the concrete floor. I probably should have at least let him help me up.

Once I got myself upright, I slid back into the hot tub to soothe the pain I'd just inflicted upon myself. How stupid was I? Did I not know the difference between a ringtone and an actual person screaming?

And why did he have a ringtone of someone screaming, anyway? What kind of person had a screaming ringtone?

I shook my head. I needed to get back up to my room and go back to bed. From the looks of things, the snowfall had slowed a bit, which meant I might actually get married in the morning.

The instant I tried to climb out of the tub, I felt the bruising down my spine. That wouldn't make wearing a lace dress any more comfortable.

I should have stayed in my room and forced myself to sleep.

With my robe wrapped around me, I headed to the women's locker room.

The lights were on automatic timers, which turned on with movement. They should have been off, but they were on. Which meant someone else was in the women's locker room.

Adrenaline pulsed through me again. I took a deep

breath. It was probably just housekeeping, and here I was freaking out.

I thought a guy was trying to drown me when he was playing a prank.

I thought a ringtone was an actual human screaming.

Since becoming a park ranger, it was like my brain was programmed to expect the worst.

The light being on was probably a fluke. Something completely innocent.

My heart rate slowed.

And then I saw her.

Eloise.

Lying in a pool of blood.

6

I rushed to her side, trying not to disturb any potential evidence.

"Eloise," I said, shaking her shoulder. Her eyelashes fluttered a bit, but she didn't gain consciousness.

I pulled my phone from my robe pocket and tried to dial 9-1-1, but the call wouldn't go through. "Dammit."

She wore the same black dress she'd had on earlier, but she was barefoot, and her hair looked like she'd repeatedly run a comb through it backward.

And the blood. There seemed to be a lot, but mixed with some of the standing water from the pool, it was hard to tell how much exactly.

"Eloise, where are you injured?" I didn't want to move her if she'd fallen and had a neck or back injury, but I also didn't want her to bleed out.

Again, her eyelashes fluttered as if she could hear me but couldn't respond. Her chest moved up and down with tiny breaths. She had no visible injuries.

"I need to call for help," I said, remembering Scott had service out by the hot tub. "I'll be right back."

I hated leaving her there, but I had no choice. "Don't go dying on me, okay?"

As I rushed from the locker room back out to the pool, I spotted a bloody knife under the sinks. She'd been stabbed. Possibly in the back. I'd have to roll her over and stop the bleeding.

I redialed 9-1-1 when I got back to the pool area, but I still had no signal. I let out a loud groan. "Come on!" I tried again, but still nothing.

Without running, I hurried back to the locker room. I grabbed a bunch of towels and rushed back to Eloise. The pool of blood around her didn't seem to be any larger than it had been before, which meant moving her to check for bleeding from her back could cause more harm than good.

I placed the rolled-up towels alongside her head to stabilize her neck in case she did gain consciousness. Her chest still moved up and down, though her breaths seemed more sporadic.

"Eloise," I said, touching her shoulder. Her skin was warm, meaning she probably hadn't been here very long. "Eloise? Can you hear me?"

This time, her eyelashes didn't flutter with recognition. I needed to get help. Fast.

"I'll be right back," I said. "Don't move, okay? If you fell, your back or neck could be messed up."

I rushed out of the locker room into the hotel. "Help! I need some help!"

Taking the stairs to the lobby two at a time, I hurried

past a giant Christmas tree toward the front desk. "Is anyone here? I need some hel—"

I ran straight into Garrett.

"Babe, what's wrong?" He held me by the shoulders and looked me up and down. "Are you hurt?"

My white robe was stained with blood—Eloise's blood. "Eloise," I said. "She's hurt. Come on."

I turned to run back down to the pool but stopped abruptly, causing Garrett to smash into the back of me, taking both of us to the floor.

"Why did you stop?" Garrett asked, his eyes wide.

"We need to call an ambulance." I pulled out my phone and glanced at the screen. "I still don't have any service. Do you?"

He pulled his phone from the pocket of his jeans and shook his head. "Doesn't look like it." He dialed anyway, but his call wouldn't connect either.

I hurried to my feet and started back down the hallway with him right behind me.

"What did you mean Eloise is hurt?" Garrett asked.

"She's in the women's locker room surrounded by blood," I said. "She's unconscious but breathing."

"And you just left her there?"

"I had to get help," I said. "I don't want to move her in case she slipped and hurt her back or neck."

The image of the knife flickered in my mind, but I didn't mention it to Garrett.

Not yet.

Right now, we needed to focus on Eloise.

Even if there was someone running around who may or may not have stabbed her.

I shook the thought from my head. It could have been a coincidence. The knife was pretty far under the sink. And if someone intentionally stabbed her, wouldn't they have taken the knife with them?

"Careful," I said, holding a hand out so Garrett wouldn't run on the slick locker room floor. "It's slick."

We walked around the corner to where Eloise had been, but she was gone.

The blood was still on the ground. The towels were still rolled up parallel to one another, just as I'd placed them alongside her head.

But Eloise wasn't there.

"Uh, Rylie?" Garrett looked back at me with questions in his eyes.

"She was right here," I said. "I put those towels next to her head to keep her from moving."

"And now she's gone?" Garrett asked.

My eyes shifted to beneath the sink.

The knife was gone too.

"Do you think she got up and walked away?" Garrett asked. "Maybe she needed to use the bathroom?"

I shook my head. "I think something bad happened—someone hurt her intentionally. Maybe they hid when I came in. They probably didn't expect me to be here so late at night. And then when I left, they took the evidence."

"As in Eloise?" Garrett checked the empty bathroom stalls.

"There was also a knife," I said.

Garrett peeked out from one of the stalls. "A knife?"

The tone of his voice made my stomach drop.

"There was a knife in here, and you thought she was bleeding out because she fell?"

"I didn't see any wounds," I said. "And the pool of blood wasn't growing as if she were bleeding."

"But you saw a knife, and now it's gone?" Garrett went back to searching the bathroom stalls, his frustration with me evident.

"Yes." At least, I thought I had. It had been a bit of a blur.

I searched the ground again. Maybe Eloise had struggled when someone tried to move her and had accidentally kicked the knife away. But then, how were the towels in precisely the same position?

There were no bloody footprints. No indications of a struggle.

So, what had happened to her?

"I'm going to check out here," I said, but Garrett didn't seem to care what I was doing. He was too busy shaking shower curtains.

The pool area was empty—the water in the hot tub and the pool as smooth as glass. The only footprints were the remains of mine from when I'd exited the hot tub and walked to the locker room. Even Scott's had dried.

"Find anything out here?" Garrett asked, coming up behind me.

"No," I said. "Why don't you check the men's locker room, and I'll check outside."

He hesitated.

"You okay?" I asked.

"What are you wearing?"

My robe had come open, revealing my swimming suit.

"What do you mean?" I asked, but when I looked down, I realized something was different with my bikini.

"Uh, is that a—"

"Penis," I said. "Someone drew a penis on my white swimming suit."

Garrett looked horrified, then snickered.

I pulled my robe back around me as Scott's words floated back into my head—*nice bikini.*

Ugh.

"I'll meet you back here in a few minutes," I said.

Garrett was obviously trying not to laugh at me as he turned toward the men's locker room.

I pushed the bar on the heavy metal door, letting a cold burst of air into the warm room. My breath came out in little puffs.

"Eloise? Are you out here?" I called.

A rock sat outside the door to prop it open, so it didn't lock people out. Probably so they could come out and smoke and then go back to swimming. I pushed the rock between the door and the jam with my foot and walked as silently as I could in flip-flops on the snowy ground.

The air was still—the clouds holding onto their snowflakes.

For now.

I could only hope they'd wait until after tomorrow or move deeper into the mountains before they released their flurries.

"Eloise?" I called again.

No answer.

Not that I expected one.

There was no sign that anyone had been out here since it had stopped snowing. The only footprints were my own.

I turned back to the door just in time to hear it close.

Either the rock slipped out, or someone had closed it purposefully.

I hurried as quickly as I could, careful not to slip again.

"Hey, open up," I yelled, banging on the metal door.

"I'm out here. I propped it open so that I could get back in."

I pressed my ear up against the door but couldn't hear anything on the other side.

The rock was on the ground next to my foot. Someone would have had to have pushed it out of the way. If it had slipped, it would have gone inside.

"Let me in!" I yelled louder. "It's really freaking cold out here!"

My knuckles hurt from banging on the door so hard.

Garrett knew I was outside. Surely, he'd open the door for me when he realized I was locked out.

But after waiting for what felt like forever, I had to find another way in.

My only option was through the snow and back around to the lobby. It would be cold, but if I ran, I'd probably make it with minimal frostbite.

I channeled my inner child, doing high knees in gym class, and took off as fast as I could.

The snow burned my skin. My flip-flops almost instantly got stuck in the heavy, wet snow, so I left them and kept moving barefoot. The robe did nothing but kept my torso covered and dragged like a heavy cape, whipping the backs of my legs with every step.

Occasionally, I'd hit a deep patch of snow and topple forward, sending my hands and arms into the frosty fluff. For the first time in my life, I hated snow.

Tears formed in my eyes, blurring my vision.

What if something had happened to Garrett, too? What if that's why he didn't open the door for me?

And what about Eloise?

And our wedding?

Everything was so messed up.

The burning sensation in my legs and feet eventually turned to numbness, making it less painful but harder to move because I couldn't feel where I was going.

I fell more frequently.

The driveway came into sight, but I still had a long way to go.

My lungs ached, and my throat felt as if I'd swallowed fire.

My nostrils stuck together as I sniffed back the snot dripping from my nose.

The tears on my cheeks felt like icicles.

Finally, I made it to the driveway where the snow wasn't as deep, though it hadn't been plowed and would be hard for most two-wheel-drive vehicles to traverse.

Who was I kidding? It wasn't like I'd be able to go forward with my wedding when I knew there was a woman in danger. Even if she was Garrett's ex who wanted him back. Especially because of that. It wouldn't be classy in the slightest.

When I reached the doors, I could barely get my hand to slip into the handle to pull it open.

Once inside, the heat burned my skin.

"Oh my God," a voice said. "What the hell are you doing?"

8

Megan stood in the lobby, gaping at me. "Are you okay?"

I couldn't form words through my chattering teeth.

"Of course, you're not okay." She hurried to my side and began rubbing my arms with her hands. "Why were you outside, in a robe and a penis bikini?"

"D-d-d-d-did y-y-you d-d-draw th-the p-p-p-penis?" I couldn't keep my body from shivering. Which was good. It was when someone stopped shivering that you needed to worry.

"Did I draw the penis? On your swimsuit?" Megan looked at me as if I'd just asked her why the sky was green. "That's what you care about right now? You're a human popsicle. We need to get you a blanket."

She hurried over to the front desk and rang the bell repeatedly.

"Is anyone here?" she called out. "We need some help."

A woman emerged from the back. Her name tag said, Carly. "I'm sorry, I was on the phone."

"The ph-ph-phone?" I said, hurrying over to them. "Call the p-police. Or an ambulance."

"Yes," Megan said. "My sister is hypothermic. We need a blanket and an ambulance."

"N-not for m-m-me." I tried to steady my jaw so I could speak without shivering. "Eloise."

"Eloise is out there too?" Megan's eyes widened.

I shook my head. "N-no. Sh-she's h-hurt."

"Where?" Megan asked while the woman hurried back into the office.

Then I realized, if I didn't know where she was, there was no way we could help her.

Maybe Garrett found her.

"The phone line is dead," Carly said, emerging with a button-down sweater. "This is mine. Wear it until I can find you a blanket."

Megan peeled the snow-drenched robe from my skin and quickly replaced it with the sweater.

"Th-thank you," I said.

"Let's get you in front of the fireplace," Megan said. "And you can tell me what happened."

"I'll get her a blanket and something warm to drink," Carly said.

Megan sat me down on one of the cozy couches in front of the roaring fireplace.

"You said Eloise is hurt, right?"

"Yes, but I don't know where she is." Finally, my teeth stopped chattering long enough for me to speak.

"Start from the beginning."

By the time I told her what had happened, Carly was back with a steaming mug of coffee and a heavy blanket. "I brought cream and sugar too."

Normally, I would have doctored it up with both, but I was too cold. I sipped the bitter liquid, letting it warm me from the inside out. "Thank you."

Megan wrapped the blanket around my legs, tucking me in. "I'm going to kill Garrett when I find him."

"He probably got sidetracked looking for Eloise," I said, then turned to Carly. "Do you know if there were any staff in the pool area who might have closed the door to the outside?"

"I'll check." She walked back to the desk and pulled out a boxy black radio.

"Can you also ask all housekeeping staff not to do any cleaning until further notice?" I asked.

Carly nodded.

"What if someone intentionally locked you out?" Megan whispered.

"Then Garrett could be in trouble too," I said.

"Unless he's the one who did it," she mumbled under her breath.

"Megan!" I gaped at her.

"What?"

"You can't possibly be suggesting my own fiancé would lock me out into the cold."

"Look," she said, glancing at where Carly was still speaking into the radio. "There's a reason I'm out of bed right now. I followed Garrett tonight."

"I'm sorry, what?" If I wasn't already warming up from the blanket and the fire and the sweater and the coffee, my speeding heart rate was sure to get my blood piping hot.

"I followed him," she said. "After he kissed Eloise—"

"She kissed him," I corrected.

"After they kissed, I wanted to know what he would do." She glanced around to make sure we were still alone. "I staked out his room, and, sure enough, he left it and went to another room. Eloise's."

"How do you know it was Eloise's room?" I asked.

"I saw her open the door." Megan's voice was apologetic.

I didn't want to ask, but I had to. "Did he go inside?"

She nodded.

"But Nathan?"

"He must not have been there," Megan said.

My mind reeled. This wasn't happening. Not now. Not right before my wedding. Garrett had promised he wouldn't see her again.

"I talked to all the staff, and no one was down in the pool tonight," Carly said.

Megan gave me a meaningful look.

"My fiancé didn't lock me out of the building," I said, though my resolve on this was a bit less after finding out he'd snuck off to Eloise's room.

Carly's eyes widened. "I'll be in the office if you need anything. And you can return the sweater whenever."

I turned back to Megan. "Look, maybe he's had a change of heart about our wedding, but he could simply call it off. He wouldn't need to literally freeze me out."

Maybe that's why he seemed so annoyed with me

when we were looking for Eloise. And why he'd forgotten to meet me back in the main pool area.

Or maybe someone had attacked him, too.

I stood to my feet and started toward the pool.

"Where are you going?" Megan asked.

"If someone locked me out, they might have hurt Garrett," I said. "I need to check on him."

My legs ached with every step. My bare feet felt like pins were shooting through them.

I could hear the screams coming from the pool before I even reached the women's locker room.

"Oh my God, is this where you found her?" Megan asked when we ran past the blood-soaked floor.

The screams got louder as we got closer. "Come on."

When we turned the corner to the pool, the source of the screaming was immediately evident.

And not at all what I expected.

9

"What in the ever-loving hell are you doing down here?" Megan yelled at her husband.

The screams we'd heard were coming from the mouths of her four boys as they splashed and dunked each other in the pool.

"The boys woke up, and you were gone. They wanted to come to the pool." Tom shrugged.

Megan did not look pleased. "Did one of you close that door?" She pointed to the door I'd taken to look outside.

"It was letting in the cold air," Chase said. "We were shivering."

"You almost killed your aunt!" Megan said.

All four of her boys, plus Tom, looked at her as if she was crazy.

I sat on the edge of the hot tub and let my feet sink into the hot water. It burned, but finally, the chill was subsiding. "Have you seen Garrett?"

"Nope," Tom said.

"Did you come through the men's locker room?" I asked.

Tom laughed. "As opposed to the women's?"

I thought about this for a second. If one of the boys had locked me out and they'd come through the men's locker room, they would have had to have seen Garrett. Unless he hadn't been looking in the men's locker room like he said he would.

"Megan, will you take me to Eloise's room?" I asked. It only made sense that he'd look for her back in her room. Especially if she'd gotten up and walked out of the women's locker room after regaining consciousness.

"You five better sleep in tomorrow," she said as we walked back into the women's locker room.

They answered her with various forms of acknowledgment.

"Love you, honey!" Tom shouted after us.

"I love you too," Megan said back to him.

"You guys are so cute together," I said. "I hope Garrett and I are like that after we've been married more than a decade."

Megan didn't reply. Whenever she didn't say something, it meant she disagreed and didn't want to start a fight.

"Maybe he went to Eloise's room earlier to get closure," I said. "Maybe it wasn't what it looked like."

"Or maybe he's the one who attacked her," Megan said. "I mean, he'd go to jail, but at least you'd know he didn't cheat on you."

"Megan!"

She winked at me. "Kidding!"

We walked the rest of the way in silence. When we arrived at Eloise's door, Megan knocked loudly, without hesitation.

When no one answered, she knocked again and shouted, "We know you're in there. Open up!"

The door swung open, and we came face to face with a very unhappy-looking woman in a green facemask, a flowery silk robe, and a matching head wrap. The woman was not Eloise.

"What are you doing out here banging on my door in the middle of the night?" Bernadette shouted.

"Why are you in Eloise's room?" Megan asked.

"This isn't Eloise's room," Bernadette said, stepping into the hall and closing the door behind her. "This is my room."

"But Eloise was here earlier," Megan said.

"Visiting her mother," Bernadette countered.

"And Garrett was here too," Megan said. "With Eloise."

"With both of us," Bernadette said.

I let out a sigh of relief. If Bernadette was in the room with them, it was unlikely anything serious happened.

"Where is Eloise now?" Megan asked.

"How should I know?" Bernadette answered. "She and Garrett left at least an hour ago."

So much for that sigh of relief.

"What room is Eloise staying in?" I asked. "We need to find her. She might be hurt or in danger."

"What do you mean Eloise is in danger?" Maybe it was the face mask, but Bernadette didn't look too terribly surprised by this information.

"Rylie found her bleeding all over the floor in the women's locker room by the pool," Megan said.

"Then why aren't you there with her?" Bernadette asked.

"When Rylie came back after looking for help, Eloise was gone," Megan said. "We thought she might have gone back to her room."

"Gone?" Bernadette narrowed her eyes at me. "You left her alone, and she disappeared?"

My insides twisted. I should never have left Eloise alone.

"Can you take us to her room?" Megan was getting impatient.

Bernadette eyed us one last time before turning and marching in the direction opposite from where we'd come.

Megan and I hurried after her.

At the end of the hall, Bernadette stopped abruptly and knocked on one of the doors.

The door swung open.

"Where is my daughter?" Bernadette pushed past Nathan into the room. "I know you did something to her."

Nathan's face was bright red and angry. "You can't just come in here and—"

"What are you doing here?" Bernadette said to someone else inside the room.

"I was looking for Eloise," Garrett answered.

Megan gave me an apologetic look.

Garrett had abandoned me outside in the cold to look for Eloise.

I'd had enough. I was cold and tired and on the verge of tears.

"I'm going to go back to my room," I said to Megan. "There are plenty of people looking for Eloise."

Garrett peeked around the corner at me. "Rylie?" He looked me up and down. "Are you okay?"

I just shook my head and walked away.

Megan must have stepped between him and the door because I heard her say, "I think you need to give her some space."

10

I hated feeling like the girl at the middle school dance storming off and crying in the bathroom, but I didn't have it in me to stay and figure things out with Garrett right now.

I needed to be alone with my thoughts. To get out of my penis bikini and into some real clothes.

My first stop was the shower. I let the warm water slowly increase my body temperature until I felt almost back to normal.

Then the exhaustion hit.

I toweled myself off and pulled on my warmest pair of sweats before climbing into my bed and immediately falling asleep.

When I woke, I had a headache the size of Alaska and a gnawing in my stomach that said I should have pushed my emotions aside to help look for Eloise last night.

My phone lay silent on my nightstand. When I checked it, there was still no service.

I fixed my hair and put on a pair of shoes before heading out to see if anyone was around.

The first person I saw was Garrett.

Asleep.

In the hallway against the wall across from my room.

When my door latched closed, his eyes opened, and he was on his feet. "Rylie," he said as if I might be a figment of his imagination.

Part of me wanted to rush to him and let him engulf me in a hug. I mean, he had slept outside my room all night.

But the other part of me was still angry he'd let me get locked outside. And that he'd been with Eloise alone last night.

"You were with her last night."

"I can explain everything," Garrett said. "I'm just so glad you're okay."

He took a step toward me, his arms open as if he wanted to hug me, but I wrapped my arms around my torso and stepped back. I didn't want his hugs. Not yet.

"Explain," I said.

"Should we get some coffee first?"

Garrett knew how grumpy I was in the morning before I had my coffee.

"Fine." I turned toward the den, and he hurried to keep up with me.

Besides one staff member manning the breakfast spread, the den was empty.

I grabbed a blueberry muffin and a mug of black coffee

before curling up into the corner of one of the couches in front of the fireplace.

Garrett grabbed his own coffee and sat in a chair opposite me.

"Before you explain anything," I said. "Did you find Eloise?"

He shook his head. "We looked everywhere we could think to look, but it's like she vanished. I tried to get in touch with the police, but all the phone lines are down, and we're officially snowed in."

One glance out the two-story window told me everything I needed to know. Snow piled up at least five feet, and it was still coming down.

I took a sip of my black coffee and winced. It was hot and bitter and matched my energy perfectly.

"We decided to stop searching for the night and go back to it today," Garrett continued. "After we had a chance to talk to you."

"Me? Why me?"

"Because you're the only person at this resort who has experience dealing with crime scenes."

I set my coffee on the stand next to me and folded my hands in my lap, trying to keep my composure. "Let me get this straight. You want me to help you find your missing ex-girlfriend on my now-canceled wedding day after you've done nothing but complain about me investigating crimes in the past?" It wasn't entirely true—he'd tried to be supportive a few times—but I was too angry to care. "Did you know that I got trapped outside in the bitter cold last night while you were off looking for her? I was in a wet bikini, flip-flops, and a robe. I could have died."

Garrett glanced down at his lap. "I feel terrible about that. Megan already chastised me for it."

"Why were you with her last night after you left my room?" I didn't know that I wanted the answer, but I needed it. "You promised you'd stay away from her."

"I saw Bernadette in the hall, and we started chatting about old times." He looked up at me with tears in his eyes. "When we got to her room, she invited me inside for a drink. I thought nothing of it. Then Eloise showed up."

I took a bite of my muffin to keep my mouth busy, so I wouldn't end up shouting at him.

"I should have left right away, but I knew nothing would happen—she wouldn't try anything—with Bernadette in the room. When I left, Eloise followed me. We didn't leave together like Bernadette apparently insinuated to you and Megan."

One thing I'd learned from being a park ranger was staying silent often led to people giving more details. Which is partially why I didn't respond. The other reason was because I was afraid of what I might say.

"She followed me," Garrett said. "And she tried to kiss me again. But this time, I was ready for it. I stopped her. And she stormed off. And then apparently got hurt. Last night, when I seemed frustrated with you, I was more frustrated with myself. If only I hadn't been so stern with her, maybe I could have walked her back to her room, and she would have been safe. That's probably why I got so tied up in looking for her. I didn't think you'd get locked outside. If I had, I never would have left."

"Did you even look in the men's locker room?" I asked.

"Yes," he said. "Quickly, but yes."

"Because my nephews and Tom didn't see you in there, and they're the ones who shut the door on me."

"We probably just missed each other," he said. "It doesn't take very long to open a few stalls and look into some empty showers."

He had a point.

"So? Will you help? With the case?" His big puppy dog eyes melted my resolve slightly.

"How do we even know there is a case?" I asked. "Maybe she slipped, cracked her head—head wounds bleed a lot and mixed with the water it probably wasn't as much blood as it looked like—then regained conscious-ness while I was gone and walked away."

"But then, where did she go?" Garrett asked.

"Did you check your room?"

Garrett's eyes widened. "You don't think she went to my room, do you?"

"I think it's entirely possible." I stood. "Maybe she wanted to apologize for being so forward."

He followed me out of the den to the elevator.

"I'm really sorry about all of this," he said when the elevator doors closed. "And I appreciate you helping with the case."

"If there's even a case."

Sure, there had been a knife. Or at least I thought there had been a knife. But maybe that had nothing to do with anything. Maybe it was a fluke. Or maybe I was seeing things. I *had* taken a fall myself.

My stomach turned when we got to Garrett's door.

Garrett looked like he might pass out.

The knife I'd been stewing about was stabbed into his door, dried blood on the blade. Hanging from the tip was a massive diamond ring.

"This—it's," Garrett reached for the heart pendant, but I stopped him.

"It's evidence," I said. "We need to treat it as such."

"It's her engagement ring." A sob rose from deep in his chest.

"I need you to open the door," I said.

"What if she's in there?" Garrett's face was getting paler by the second.

"Come here." I grabbed his arm and took him to the other side of the hall, his back against the wall. "Bend down, put your head between your knees, and take deep breaths."

I took the key card from his hand. "I'll look in your room."

Careful not to touch the knife or the ring, I swiped the card and opened the door.

His room was pristine. Almost as if the maid had come in, though I knew that wasn't the case. Garrett was just a very tidy person.

I opened the closet to find his clothes neatly hung and his empty suitcase sitting at the bottom. The bathroom, though used, was still nearly spotless, with a single towel hung on the rod and his products in a tidy bundle on the counter.

His bed was made—differently from how the maids had made the beds.

But, most importantly, there was no sign of Eloise.

"She's not in there," I said, exiting the room.

Garrett was slumped over on the floor.

"What happened to him?" Bernadette asked, walking down the hall toward me. "And who's not in there?"

"We were looking for Eloise," I said.

"And Garrett thought it would be a good time to take a nap?" Bernadette asked.

"He probably passed out." I knelt beside him and shook his shoulder. "Garrett? Wake up."

His eyes fluttered open. "What happened?"

"I think you passed out," I said. "I didn't find Eloise in your room."

"Why would Eloise be in Garrett's room?" Bernadette asked. "Unless—"

"No," Garrett said, cutting her off. "No unless. She's never been in my room."

"Not this one anyway," Bernadette mumbled loudly enough to be heard.

I did my best not to roll my eyes. "This might be more serious than we thought." I stood and pointed to the knife and ring on the door.

"Is that Eloise's engagement ring?" Bernadette's eyes widened. "But she never took that off."

"Don't touch it," I said. "It might be evidence."

"It's more than evidence," Bernadette said. "It looks like a warning."

I considered the knife protruding from the door. If it was a warning, what was it warning us about?

"I had no idea how serious this was," Bernadette said. "I thought maybe Eloise was going through another one of her dramatic phases like she used to as a child. Going missing to prove no one cared about her. But she never would have left the ring behind."

"Unless she thought it was the only way to get Garrett to care," I said.

Bernadette narrowed her eyes and took a step toward me. "My daughter doesn't need to go to this extent to get a man to care about her. She's perfectly happy with Nathan."

"Then why does she keep making passes at my fiancé?" I asked.

Garrett got to his feet. "That's enough arguing. We're not helping anything by arguing like this."

"Let's check in with Nathan," I said. "I'm sure he's

been up all night looking for her. Maybe he found something."

We walked in silence to Nathan and Eloise's room.

I knocked, and Nathan almost immediately opened the door, looking well-rested and refreshed.

"Did you find her?" I asked.

He shook his head. "I looked all night, but she's just gone. I don't know that there's much else we can do."

"Did you know Eloise was hitting on Garrett?" Bernadette pushed past me to come face to face with Nathan. "Is that why you killed her?"

Nathan looked at Bernadette as if she was insane. "Will you stop saying I killed Eloise?"

"But you did know they kissed," I said. "You saw them."

"I thought I was well-hidden in that closet," he said. "I admit, I saw them. But Eloise has always been someone who wants what she can't have. I've known that since before I proposed."

"And you're just okay with that?" I asked.

He shrugged. "She was fickle. It didn't mean she didn't love me."

"Why are you speaking about her in the past tense?" Bernadette asked.

It was a good catch.

"I didn't realize I was," Nathan said, unaffected by the way everything looked.

"Come on, man," Garrett said from behind me. "What'd you do to her?"

"I didn't do anything," he said. "Why do you think

something happened to her? Maybe Rylie is just making all this up."

"I saw the blood in the locker room," Garrett said, pushing past Bernadette and me. "And the knife and the ring. Now, you'll tell me what you know, or I'll beat you into next week."

I'd never seen Garrett so worked up. His fists were clenched at his sides, and a vein protruded from his neck.

"Last night, Eloise and I got into an argument about the kiss," Nathan said. "I told her she needed to decide what she wanted. She stormed out and said she needed to talk to her mother. That's the last I saw of her."

"And you didn't lay a hand on her?" I asked. "Because you seemed pretty angry outside our rehearsal dinner dining room."

"I'd never hurt Eloise," he said. "Frankly, she's not worth going to jail over."

This sent Garrett into motion. He launched himself at Nathan, tackling him to the floor.

Nathan let out a high-pitched scream as he tried to hit Garrett off him.

Garrett sat up and drew a fist back as if he was going to punch Nathan straight in the nose.

"Garrett, stop!" I grabbed his arm before he could release his punch. "Don't do this!"

Bernadette ran out of the room, screaming for help.

Garrett looked back at me, and his face softened.

Nathan peeked between his arms which covered his face.

I let go of Garrett's arm and took a step back.

Garrett got off of Nathan, and Nathan scrambled to his feet.

"You have issues," Nathan said. "I don't know why Eloise or Rylie or anyone else would want to be with you so badly. I mean, sure, you have a great body and make a lot of money, but other than that."

I shook my head.

"Garrett, go out and get Bernadette to stop yelling," I said. "I need to speak to Nathan alone."

Garrett looked at me as if I was crazy for even suggesting being alone with Nathan.

"It's okay," I said. "We'll be just fine."

Garrett reluctantly turned and walked out the door.

I turned to Nathan. "I didn't want to ask you this in front of Garrett because I have a feeling I know the answer, and it might send Garrett into another fit of rage."

Nathan said nothing.

"Did you even look for Eloise last night?"

Nathan stared at me for a moment. "Yes."

"But not for long, right?"

"Look," Nathan said. "You don't know Eloise as I do. She's a pain in the ass. She does things like this all the time. Goes missing. Waits to see if people care. Then throws it in their faces when they don't. I told her the last time I wouldn't do it again. And I'm not."

"But she was hurt," I said. "I saw her unconscious lying in blood."

"Was she truly unconscious? Did you pinch her?"

I gaped at him. I never thought to check if she was faking it.

"What about the ring and the knife?" I asked. "We

found her engagement ring stuck to Garrett's door with a knife."

"It's staged," he said. "Maybe she's trying to get Garrett to care about her again. Or maybe when she went to find him, and he wasn't in his room, she got angry. Don't worry. She won't want him once she has him. She just wants to know she can still get him."

"And you're okay with all of this?" I asked.

"No," he said. "But what choice do I have?"

"There are plenty of women in this world," I said. "You don't have to be with Eloise."

"Oh, you're right about that," he said. "I just meant it's not like I can leave now. Not with all the snow. But once it clears, you better bet I'm out of here."

"You're going to call off your engagement?"

"Wouldn't you?" he asked. "Honestly, I'm surprised you're not calling off yours."

"Why would you say that?"

"Didn't we both see the same kiss?" Nathan smiled. "Garrett might have stopped it, but not very quickly."

I thought back to the kiss. Was Nathan trying to get in my head, or had Garrett lingered in the kiss?

"This isn't about my relationship," I said, stopping that train of thought. "This is about finding Eloise. Maybe she's making all of this up, but what if she's not? What if she's really hurt?"

"I guess she shouldn't have cried wolf so many times."

"That's not acceptable," I said. "You need to help us look. You may not want to marry her anymore, but you're the one who knows her best. Is there anyone who might want to hurt Eloise?"

"How long do you have?" He rolled his eyes and dramatically stood from the bed. "Fine, I'll help. But not because I want to marry her anymore. Only because I'm already bored with being trapped in this stupid hotel, and this will help pass the time."

Did he really think she was hiding, or was he hiding something? Maybe this entire act was a cover to disguise his real actions.

"Why don't you tell me exactly what you did last night," I said. "One more time."

"Eloise and I fought after she and Garrett kissed. She stormed out, and I went to sleep."

"Wait, I thought you said you looked for her," I said.

"I lied," he said with a shrug. "I went to bed and slept like a baby."

I had to take a deep breath to keep from launching myself at him like Garrett had before. This guy was a total jerk.

"Let's go," I said. "You're going to help us look for her. *Now.*"

Garrett, Bernadette, Nathan, and I walked silently back to the den where a bunch of people had assembled—all of them there for my wedding.

"There you are," Mom said, rushing to me. "Megan told me what happened last night. Why didn't you get me? I could have helped. I could have run you a bath or gotten you warm towels or—"

"Mom, stop. It's okay. I'm okay."

She pulled me into a tight hug, and I had to fight the tears that wanted to spill down my cheeks. There was something about a mother's hug that did that to a child. A mother's arms were one of the safest places in the world.

"But I will need your help to find Eloise." I raised my voice. "Could everyone listen up for a minute?"

Our friends and family turned to me with smiles on their faces.

"Last night, Eloise—Garrett's friend—went missing," I

said. "I found her in the women's locker room unconscious and surrounded by blood."

A few people gasped.

"But when I went to get help because my cell phone had no service, she disappeared."

"Like a ghost?" Chase said.

"Or a genie?" Bryce said with a giggle.

"Shh," Megan said to her boys. "Let Rylie finish."

"What I meant to say was, she was gone when I got back to the locker room. Then, this morning, Garrett and I found her engagement ring hanging from a bloody knife stabbed into Garrett's hotel room door."

"Whoa," Alex said.

Megan gave him a warning look.

He and his brothers snickered.

"I'd like to ask for your help," I continued. "Since the wedding has to be postponed because of the incredible amount of snow we've gotten, maybe we can use our time to find Eloise."

"Do you think we're in danger?" Selena asked, pulling her baby closer to her chest.

"I can't be sure," I said. "If someone did hurt Eloise, then possibly."

"Why if?" Dad asked. "Isn't it pretty apparent someone did?"

"There are many possibilities, but the most likely is that someone hurt her," I said. "Which means we need to stay with someone else at all times. Don't go wandering off by yourself. And keep your children in your sight."

"Why would someone want to hurt Eloise?" Selena asked.

"Why wouldn't someone want to hurt her?" Nathan said under his breath.

I could see Garrett tense up from the corner of my eye.

"We don't know at the moment." I glanced around. Someone in this room could be the person who hurt Eloise. In fact, it was likely the person was in the room. I took a deep breath. "But just as soon as we get cell service, we will call out to the police, and they can take over the investigation."

"Why don't we simply wait until we can contact the police?" Mom asked, worry in her voice.

"Because Eloise might still be okay. And if she is, we want to make sure she stays that way," I said.

Garrett reached over and took my hand, squeezing it in his.

"Where do we start?" Tom asked, standing from the back of the couch where he was perched.

"Megan," I said. "Where did you look last night?"

"We searched all the hallways, the locker rooms, the pool area, the gym, the meeting rooms, and all the public spaces," Megan said. "I suppose since it's daytime, we could start going room to room to see who else might be here."

"I've asked the housekeeping staff to hold off on cleaning anything," I said. "Just in case there's evidence to preserve."

Several people nodded.

"That's ridiculous," Bernadette said from beside me. "I need my turndown service. I'm paying top dollar here."

"I understand your frustration," I said.

"Why don't you just search her room? When it's

cleared, you can tell the staff they can clean it," Nathan said.

"Search my room?" Bernadette asked. "That's preposterous. There's no reason she'd need to search my room. I'd never do anything to hurt my own daughter."

My mind went back to the previous night when Megan and I had shown up at Bernadette's door. She'd been pretty quick to close it behind her and join us in the hall in her robe and face mask.

"Do you have something to hide?" Megan asked, beating me to it.

Bernadette pulled her sweater around her more tightly and crossed her arms over her chest. "Absolutely not. But that's beside the point."

"Is it, though?" I asked. "The way I see it, everyone is a suspect until proven innocent."

"What about you?" Bernadette asked, pointing a finger at me. "You're the one whose entire relationship was falling apart because of my daughter's presence. Maybe you hurt her and made this whole story up to clear your name."

"Search my room," I said. "I have nothing to hide."

Apparently, my insistence they search my room meant the entire group of people from the den could do so.

"What is this?" Mom held up the bikini I'd been wearing the night before.

"It's a pee-pee," Devin said as his older brothers giggled behind him.

I snatched it away from her and shoved it into the trash.

"I thought the drawing was rather good," Megan whispered. "And to answer your question, yep, it was me. I thought you'd wear it to your bachelorette party."

"And when exactly was I going to have a bachelorette party?" I asked.

"I'd planned on doing it last night, but since no one could get here because of the snow, I had to postpone it."

"Will you be offended if I don't wear the penis bikini to my bachelorette party?" I asked. "Assuming we still have one?"

She smiled, but before she could reply, Nathan yelled out, "What is this?"

He held a necklace with what looked like a loop or a ring on it.

And it was covered in blood.

"What is it?" Megan asked.

"It's her engagement ring," Garrett said.

Nathan laughed. "I think you're mistaken. The ring I gave her was far larger than that little band."

"Not the one you gave her," Garrett said, reaching for the ring. "The one I did. She wore it on a chain around her neck after she declined my proposal."

Nathan dropped the ring and the chain in Garrett's hand.

"You stayed together after she said no to your proposal?" I asked.

"Not for long," Garrett said. "I thought if she kept the ring, it might get her to change her mind."

"You're telling me that stupid band she wears around her neck was the ring you proposed with?" Nathan asked.

Garrett didn't take his eyes off the ring. "Yeah. I guess so."

"But why is it here? In your room?" Nathan asked me.

Shit.

I'd been too worried about how Garrett was staring at that ring to realize the implications. "I have no idea. Where exactly did you find it?"

Nathan pointed inside the drawer in my nightstand. "In here."

Garrett looked from where Nathan was pointing to me. "Rylie?"

"I don't know how that got in there," I said. "Maybe he planted it there."

Garrett turned back to Nathan. "Did you?"

"Between the two of us, which do you think would want Eloise gone more? Me—the man Eloise had no problem cheating on—or the woman whose man was about to leave her for Eloise?"

"I wasn't about to leave Rylie for Eloise," Garrett said.

"Then you won't mind if I take the ring," Nathan said, holding out a hand.

Garrett looked torn.

"For goodness' sake," Bernadette stepped in when Garrett didn't decide right away. "I'll take the ring. She is my daughter."

"Actually," I said. "I should take it and keep it as evidence."

"Right," Nathan said. "Or so you can destroy it, so you won't be implicated in Eloise's disappearance."

"Do you think I would have let an entire group of people go through all of my things—search every part of my hotel room—if I knew that was in my nightstand?" I shook my head. "I can see why you'd want to pin this on me. I am the easiest target. But I'm not stupid. If I committed a crime, I'd make sure no one ever knew."

My mom slapped a hand over her mouth as she gasped.

"Not that I'd commit a crime," I said, my tone exasperated. "I'm just saying."

"You did it, didn't you?" Bernadette shoved a finger into Nathan's nose. "You killed her and tried to frame Rylie."

Nathan threw his hands in the air. "I don't have to take this from you wannabe cops. Let me know when the real cops get here. In the meantime, I'll be waiting for service so I can call my lawyer." He stormed past me and out of the room.

The search of my room finished with no one finding anything else.

"Your room next?" I asked Bernadette.

"This wasn't a tit for tat," she said. "Just because you allowed them to search your room doesn't mean I want a herd of people I don't know going through my things. For all I know, they could be thieves."

"Then it'll just be me," I said. "Or Megan and me."

Bernadette eyed my sister and me. "Fine. But Garrett has to come too."

"Okay, new plan," I said, addressing the rest of the people who had just exited my room. Tom had taken the boys back to their room so they wouldn't get into any additional trouble—or lock anyone out in the freezing cold. Selena had gone back upstairs to drop the baby off with the nanny, but she was back at Cedric's side. The only other person missing was Scott.

"Has anyone seen Scott?" I asked.

Everyone looked around as if they hadn't noticed he was missing.

"He didn't come out of his room this morning when I knocked," Hugo said.

"I saw him last night at the pool," I said. "Did anyone see him after he left the pool?"

No one spoke up.

"Hugo," I said, "why don't you, Cedric, and Selena

start with his room and then keep going down the halls to each door. Find out if anyone has seen Eloise since last night. If they'll let you search their rooms, do so, but leave any obvious evidence for the police after you take photographs."

"Megan, Garrett, Bernadette, and I are going to go look at her room," I continued. "Mom, could you and Dad go to the front desk and speak with Carly to see if she can give you a master key and a list of unoccupied rooms? Then you can search those too. Oh, and this is her sweater. Tell her thank you for me."

"I'll do that," Mom said.

"And Dad, can you keep trying to get a line out to the police? This is something they should do, but I already feel bad about sleeping last night. I should have been looking for her."

"We looked last night," Megan said. "You got maybe three hours of sleep after almost freezing to death. You need to be easier on yourself."

When I looked to Garrett for his agreement with what she'd said, I was met with a frown.

My stomach dropped.

"I'll keep calling the police," Dad said. "And, Rylie, no matter what happens, none of this is your fault. You didn't hurt her. It wasn't your job to protect her. You can't be everyone's savior all the time. Sometimes, you have to take care of yourself."

He squeezed me on the shoulder and gave Garrett a meaningful look before walking away hand-in-hand with Mom.

"Come on," Bernadette said. "Let's get this over with."

Garrett and Bernadette walked ahead of Megan and me down the hallway. Megan grabbed my arm and held me back, then whispered, "Did you kill her?"

"Me?" I asked. "No!"

"Then how did the bloody necklace get into your room?"

"You can't possibly be questioning whether I killed someone right now."

She shrugged. "I would have wanted to kill her if I were you."

"We don't even know that she's dead," I said. "She might still be alive. In fact, maybe she set this all up to make us think she's dead so she could ruin my wedding."

"That sounds extreme, don't you think?"

I shrugged. "Nathan didn't seem to think so. Even Bernadette alluded to it. But we can't be sure she's dead until we find the body."

Megan followed me silently for a few seconds then said, "If you did kill her, I got your back."

"I didn't kill her," I said through gritted teeth.

"Okay," Megan said, holding her hands up. "Forget I asked."

Outside her room, Bernadette fumbled with her keycard. "I still think it's absurd you are searching my room," she said, her volume rising on the last few words. "You should search Nathan's room." She inserted the card backward, took it out, and then upside down.

"Or Garrett's," she practically shouted.

"We've looked in both of those rooms," I said. "Just open the door."

"My key isn't working, for some reason," Bernadette said, jiggling the door handle.

I rolled my eyes. "Maybe try putting it in right side up. Look at the arrow."

She slid it in correctly, but only halfway. "Maybe we need to go to the front desk and see if they have another key."

"Why are you shouting?" Garrett asked. "We're all right here."

I had a feeling why she was being so loud but didn't want to voice my suspicion in case I was wrong.

What if I was right? What if Eloise was hiding in Bernadette's room? Alive?

Would Garrett be so relieved to see her that he'd forget about me? Or would he simply have closure and be able to move forward with our wedding?

Would I be able to?

"Here." Megan yanked the key card out of Bernadette's hand. "Let me try."

When Megan got it to unlock on the first try, Bernadette pushed her way through the door in front of all of us. "It's not what it looks like."

Whatever it looked like, it wasn't what I expected.

The two queen-sized beds were destroyed—their blankets and pillows strewn around the room.

"I don't understand," Megan said. "Is this why you were worried about having people in your room? Because it's messy?"

Bernadette's gaze shifted around the room, not landing anywhere specific for any amount of time.

"Is someone in here?" I finally asked. "Is that why you were speaking so loudly?"

Bernadette didn't answer.

I opened the bathroom door and let myself inside. It was an absolute disaster. But even behind the shower curtain, no one was there.

"Check in the closet," I said.

"Already did," Megan said. "No one."

"What about behind the curtains?" I asked, coming back out.

Bernadette backed up toward the curtains, stretching her arms wide. "No. You can't look."

Garrett took a step toward her. "If you're hiding Eloise in your room, we need to know."

"Eloise?" Bernadette shook her head. "No. It's not. But you can't—"

It was too late. Garrett picked Bernadette up like the enormous bags of dog food we bought for Fizzy and

Babbitt with one arm and swiped the curtains open with the other.

A very naked man stood cupping his hands over his package like soccer players did when they were guarding a penalty kick.

"Scott?" Garrett asked.

I hadn't recognized him before with the shock of seeing a naked man behind her curtains, but now I did.

"That's why he didn't come out of his room this morning when Hugo knocked," I said. "You're sleeping with Scott?"

Garrett put a struggling Bernadette back on the ground.

"Dude, a little privacy?" Scott said.

"Dude, your ass is pressed up against the window," Garrett said.

"Nobody's down there." Scott looked behind him. "Except that party planner guy." He waved.

Garrett let the curtains go.

Bernadette sat on the bed. "I feel terrible that I was up here with him when my daughter was out there being attacked. I just didn't want the entire world to know. I figured he'd be gone by now, though."

"I only woke up when I heard you yelling at the door," Scott said. "Can you hand me my pants?"

Garrett found a pair of jeans that looked much too long for Bernadette's short legs and handed them to his friend behind the curtain.

When Scott emerged, Garrett said, "I thought you had a thing for Eloise's sister, not her mom."

"I guess the good looks run in the family," Scott winked at Bernadette.

"It's a good thing you're cute," Bernadette said. "Because you're dumber than a box of rocks. Eloise's sister is not my daughter. She's my ex-husband's daughter."

"That's good," Scott said. "She'd be pissed if she found out I slept with her mom."

"Do you still want to search my room?" Bernadette asked. "I assure you Eloise has not been here since she and Garrett left last night."

I ignored the dig and turned to Scott. "Did you see Eloise at all last night or anyone else around the pool area or down the hallways?"

Scott thought about it for a minute, then said, "Nope. Just you."

Bernadette glared at me.

"Before you say anything," I said. "I didn't hurt Eloise. Scott saw me in the hot tub."

"She thought I was trying to drown her." Scott laughed.

"It's a normal thought when someone holds your head beneath the water as you struggle," I said.

"Dude," Garrett said. "What the hell?"

"It was a joke," Scott said. "She looked so serene floating on top of the water. I wanted to cannonball in, but I didn't want to hurt her."

"So you held her under the water instead?" Megan asked. "Sounds sketchy to me. Maybe you hurt Eloise and then saw Rylie and thought you'd take care of her, too. But when she fought back, you acted like it was all a joke. You probably could have taken Eloise with her teeny tiny frame, but Rylie's thick." She turned to me. "In the best way. Like strong thick. Not fat. You're not fat."

I waved a hand in the air. "You're fine."

Garrett grabbed Scott by both shoulders and pushed him up against the curtains. "Did you do something to Eloise?"

Scott shook his head. "I like Eloise. She's much better than Rylie. I told you that yesterday."

Garrett didn't loosen his grip. "Did you try to hurt Rylie?"

"It was a joke," he said. "I didn't hurt or try to hurt anyone."

"It's fine," I said. "I'm fine."

Garrett let him go and marched past me to the door. "I need some fresh air."

Bernadette raised her eyebrows at Megan and me.

"I think we'll still have a look around," I said.

"But the only thing I was hiding was him," Bernadette said. "Isn't embarrassing me with this enough for you?"

Megan started looking through drawers. "Ugh. Don't look in that one." She slammed it shut.

Bernadette's face turned bright red.

"We'll make it quick," I said, double-checking the closet. It was empty besides the hotel-owned hangers.

"I think I'm going to head back to my room, Bernie," Scott said, kissing her on the cheek. "Let's do it again sometime."

Bernadette watched as he walked away and then sat on the edge of the bed. "This is stupid. You won't find anything."

She was right. We searched that room from top to bottom and found absolutely nothing that implicated Bernadette in Eloise's disappearance.

We let ourselves out after promising not to disclose her relationship with Scott.

"Now what?" Megan asked.

I tipped my head back and rubbed my neck, contemplating what the next move was. If Luke were here, what would he do?

Then I saw the camera. "We need to check the camera footage."

"Maybe the entire thing was caught on camera," I said.

"In the women's locker room?" Megan looked at me, horrified.

"I'm certain they don't have cameras in the locker rooms," I said. "But they might in the hallways."

"Where do you think they keep the camera footage?" Megan asked.

"By Blake's office," I said. "The door was open on one of our tours. I saw a bunch of tv monitors. If we're going to find anything, we'll find it there."

The security office would typically have been locked, but the door was wide open when we got there. And it was no surprise as to why.

"The screens are all turned off," Megan said. "Does that mean the cameras are too?"

I glanced around the room to find the switch to turn them back on. "Maybe this will do it."

I reached for the switch but quickly pulled my finger

back. The switch had blood on it. And when I looked more closely, there was blood on more than just the switch. Blood covered most of the panel. Whoever had turned this off had pressed basically every button. Which meant they probably deleted whatever footage had been recorded.

"Why aren't you pressing the button?" Megan asked.

"There's blood everywhere," I said. "Whoever did this did it in a hurry. Let's just hope they weren't successful in deleting the recordings. Maybe they turned the cameras off after everything went down."

"How will we know?"

I picked up the receiver to a landline phone, hoping to get a dial tone, but it beeped as if there was no signal. If only I could talk to Blake. "Has the cell service come back yet?"

Megan pulled out her phone and shook her head. "Not yet."

"This storm is a serious problem." I thought about it for a moment. "But whoever did this wouldn't have known the storm would be this kind of problem. Which might help us."

"How?"

"Whoever did this is trapped here, just like the rest of us," I said. "And so is Eloise—regardless of what happened to her."

"Maybe whoever did this was doing you a favor. Or trying to," Megan said. "I'm sure Garrett wouldn't shed many tears if someone took out Luke."

Her words were like a gut punch. I couldn't imagine Luke dying. Even if we were just friends, he still meant a lot to me.

Just like Eloise did to Garrett. "If the only way Garrett was going to marry me was to physically remove Eloise from the picture, I don't want to marry him, anyway."

Megan shrugged. "Fair enough."

"I'll try to get these cameras going," I said. "Even if they haven't caught what happened up until now, we need them to record what happens from now on."

"But what about the blood?" Megan asked.

I pulled my sleeve over my hand and held it up to show her. "I might get blood on my hoodie, but at least my fingerprints won't be there."

When the switch flipped on, the screens lit up one by one. Each of the cameras showed a unique part of the hotel.

"They probably didn't expect us to catch on so quickly," Megan said.

"Which might mean we can catch up with them." I did everything I could to make sure the screens were recording—I mean, a red light was on, so surely they were. "Let's check in with the others. I think we need to gather as many people as we can—including the staff."

Megan yawned. "Sorry," she said. "I think the adrenaline is wearing off a bit."

I yawned too. "I'm tired too, but I don't think there's any way I'm going to sleep with everything going on."

"Same," Megan said.

We walked back into the den where Cedric, Selena, Mom, and Dad stood huddled together.

"Did you find anything?" I asked.

"Nothing," Cedric said. "Everyone who answered the

door let us in, but their rooms were clear. What do you think we should do next?"

"Someone messed with the cameras," I said. "It seems whoever did this had a plan. I don't think they planned on a big snowstorm, though. Meaning, they probably thought they could get away, but the snow might have kept them here."

"Bernadette got here on a snowmobile," Selena said. "Maybe they left on one too."

"That was hours ago," Megan countered. "I'd guess it won't be so easy to come and go at this point."

We all glanced at the darkened windows. I checked the time on my phone.

"You may have a point," I said. "It should be light out, but those windows are completely dark."

Cedric walked to the windows and tried to see out. "They're covered in snow. I bet if we could get the doors open, it would be above my head."

Cedric wasn't a short guy in the least. This storm would definitely rival the one we'd had when I was in high school.

"I think I should take over the investigation," Bernadette said, walking up behind me with Garrett following behind her. She had on a completely different outfit and looked like she was out of breath.

Everyone began talking at once.

"Um, no," Megan said.

"Rylie can handle it," Garrett said.

"You're too close to the situation," Cedric said.

"Be my guest," I said.

Heads turned to look at me as if I was crazy.

"What?" I asked. "I thought I made myself clear that I was tired of investigating. And I thought that's what you wanted."

Garrett looked torn. "It is. I mean, I do. But what if something's wrong with Eloise?"

"Something *is* wrong with her," I said. "Either she's genuinely injured, or she's causing a fuss for the sheer drama of it all."

"You're not serious about letting her take over the investigation, are you?" Megan asked.

"Bernadette," I said. "What do you propose we do next?"

Megan gaped at me.

Garrett turned to look at Bernadette.

"I—well—I think we should keep looking for her," Bernadette said, obviously uncomfortable being put on the spot.

"We've searched practically the entire hotel," Cedric said. "And found nothing."

"Then we'll search outside," Bernadette said. "Maybe we can find some footprints."

"Doubtful," Megan said. "With the snow falling so quickly, any footprints have likely been covered by now."

"If we can get outside at all," Selena added.

"If someone took her outside," I said. "Her body might be covered with snow as well. And if that's the case, we might not find her until spring."

I plopped down on one of the couches. Just the thought of how big the challenge might be to find a body in six-plus feet of snow made me want to curl up and go back to bed.

"We can't think that way," Bernadette said. "We have to be positive. There are other buildings on this property. Maybe they took her somewhere else."

"Without getting any blood anywhere?" Megan asked.

"Maybe the blood was a deterrent to keep us focused here," I said, reluctantly getting back to my feet. "And if so, Bernadette may be onto something."

"That's fine and dandy," Megan said. "But how are we going to get to the other buildings?"

"Snowshoes?" I asked.

"Yes!" Garrett said, a renewed excitement in his eyes. "The rental hut is just outside by the pool!"

I turned to Bernadette. "Shall we gather the troops and see what we can find?"

She smiled. "We shall."

16

Everyone looked tired but seemed determined to help us find Eloise. Even Megan's kids wanted to join the search party.

"Do you think that's a good idea?" I asked, thinking about them coming across a dead body and being scarred for life.

"They'll end up getting cold five minutes after we go outside, will want to come back in, sit by the fire, and drink hot cocoa," Megan said. "So yeah, it'll be all right."

I shrugged. She was their mother, not me.

The snow hadn't completely covered the door that led to the pool, likely because of the awning over top, but it wouldn't be long before it was covered.

"We have to make this quick," I said to the people in the hallway behind me. "We don't want to get stuck outside in this weather if the door gets snowed in."

"How about Cedric and I stay here and work on clearing around the doorway," Garrett said. "That way, there's no chance we'll be stuck outside."

"Okay," I said. "And does everyone have their key cards in case the door is on a timer, and it locks us out?"

All the heads nodded.

"We'll go to the hut first to get the snowshoes, then we'll head off in teams of two or more," I said, then looked at Bernadette, who seemed to approve. "Whether or not you find anything, we'll meet back in the lobby before sundown."

The snow was the heavy wet kind, which made it hard to shovel but would make snowshoeing pretty easy.

In the distance, I could see several buildings—cabins and an event center—that we'd toured as part of the wedding options. Our wedding wasn't big enough to necessitate the event center, and we chose to stay in the main lodge, so we didn't make people walk back and forth in the snow.

But through the flurry, I could see smoke coming from the chimneys of several cabins. "Each team will take one of the cabins," I said as we plodded through the deep snow, growing deeper by the minute. "We need to introduce ourselves to whoever is inside, taking in any details we might glean. Do they seem nervous? Are they willing to let us inside? Basically, all the things you probably did when going room to room."

"There weren't many people staying in the rooms," Selena said. "I think in total, we came across maybe five rooms occupied that had nothing to do with your wedding or Eloise."

"Were there many here for Eloise?" I asked, confused. Why would anyone be there for her when she was simply visiting to look over the place?

"Just her mom, her sister, and hers," Helen said.

"Wait, Courtney's here?" Scott asked.

I glanced back at Bernadette, who looked pissed that Scott was so excited to hear about Courtney.

I turned back to Scott. "Tell me more about Courtney."

If this girl was an illegitimate daughter, she might have a motive to kill the single legitimate one.

"She's super hot," he said, oblivious to Bernadette's feelings. "We dated for a while. She's the reason Eloise knew Garrett would be here this weekend. I may have let it slip."

Scott didn't like me. He'd said no more than three words to me before this weekend. Garrett had even told me to stay away from him. He didn't think I was worthy of Garrett.

"Other than being super hot—and the fact that you tried to sabotage my wedding . . ." I gave him the opportunity to refute this.

He just shrugged.

"What else can you tell me?" I tried to keep the frustration from my voice. "Did she have a beef with Eloise? Could she be responsible for this?"

Both Scott and Bernadette spoke at the same time.

"No way," Scott said.

"Definitely," Bernadette said. "In fact, if I would have known she was here, I would have suspected her from the beginning."

Scott looked at her with an open mouth and a face full of shock.

"What?" Bernadette said with a shrug.

Megan nudged me before I could ask a follow-up question. "We need to get this show on the road. The sun will only be out so long, and it's pretty cold just standing here."

I had so many things I needed to know about Courtney, but maybe it'd be best if I spoke to her directly.

Scott led the way to the oversized supply hut that kept swimming gear in the summer and snowshoeing and cross-country skiing gear in the winter. The path had already been cleared to make room for the door to swing outward. And on the ground was something I hadn't wanted to find. Something Scott had almost stepped on.

"Please tell me that's not what I think it is," I said.

Megan came up beside me. "That looks like an ear to me."

"A what?" Bernadette squealed behind me. "Oh, God. Please tell me that's not . . ." She reached down and picked it up before I could stop her. "This is Eloise's earring."

A small heart earring made of tiny diamonds poked through the lobe.

"I bought the pair for her the day she told me about Nathan." Bernadette sniffled.

"Can I see it?" I asked, holding out a hand. Thankfully, we were all wearing gloves.

Bernadette pulled it into her chest as if she was protecting a baby bird from a hungry fox. "What do you want with her ear?"

"It's evidence," I said gently. "Can you tell if it's frozen or if it's still pliable?"

Scott gagged behind me.

"If you're going to vomit, go somewhere else," I said to him. "I think we may have found a second crime scene."

Bernadette held the ear out to me. "I want it back when you're done."

"Why do you want someone's ear?" Megan asked.

"Not the ear," Bernadette snapped. "The earring."

The ear was pliable in my hand. It hadn't been out here all night, which meant we might be in for quite the surprise when we walked into the hut.

"How about I go in alone first," I said, steeling myself for what I might find.

No one objected as I turned the handle and walked inside.

The lights flipped on, revealing a perfectly normal-looking hut. Equipment was organized nicely on the shelves—everything in its place. No dead bodies or pieces of dead bodies to be seen.

I walked around the back of the counter to look more closely. How would the ear have gotten outside the door if whoever it had come off wasn't inside? Unless it had fallen out of someone's pocket or something.

I turned back to look at the people standing behind me. Did any look suspicious? Could someone in the search party know exactly what happened to Eloise but were going through with the search to hide their guilt? Scott had been walking ahead of me.

"Oh no, the body's in here," I said. "No one come in."

Bernadette screamed, "Eloise!"

Scott full-on vomited.

Megan rushed inside. "What are you talking about?"

I watched as everyone reacted, but no one seemed to know I was lying.

"Sorry, just a pile of clothes. I was wrong," I said. "You okay, Bernadette? Scott?"

I felt terrible for lying, but I wanted to see if maybe someone would yell, *"The body's not in there!"* and then I would know who was guilty.

"Don't scare me like that again," Bernadette said. "I'm only hanging on by a thread as it is."

"If you want to investigate this case, you have to be stronger than that," I said.

"Maybe I should leave the investigation to you," she said.

I did my best not to smile. "Let's get some snowshoes so we can head out."

17

Bernadette headed off reluctantly with Scott while Megan and I went in the opposite direction. Her boys followed after us—not heading back inside for cocoa as Megan had predicted.

"Guys, if I tell you to stop, you have to listen, okay?" I asked as they followed right behind Megan like wild little ducklings.

"Why? Because we're going to see a dead body?" Devin said, his eyes wide.

"Who told you that?" Megan asked. "Alex?"

"It wasn't me," Alex said.

"I heard the gornops talking about it," Devin said.

"Grownups," Bryce corrected.

I sighed. I'd insisted kids be allowed at the wedding when Garrett had requested it be adult-only. I couldn't imagine my nephews not being present. In fact, it surprised me he was so okay with his nieces and nephews not being there.

But now, I was starting to wish we'd gone with his plan.

If we found a body with its ear—and who knew what else—cut off, they'd be scarred for life.

"Guys?" I asked again. "Can you stop if I ask you to?"

Alex raised his arm to salute me, and the other three followed suit.

"Good boys." I smiled.

We knocked on three cabin doors before someone answered. The first two were likely uninhabited, as there was no smoke coming from the chimneys and the lights were all off. But the third definitely had someone inside.

I must have stood outside for fifteen minutes knocking as someone inside seemed to be moving the furniture around.

"You need to open this door immediately," I said as loudly as I could without practically screaming. I knew they could hear me. I turned back to the boys. "Now is the time to stay back. When someone opens this door, I do not want you four to come inside, okay?"

They all nodded.

"In fact, why don't you stay outside too," I said to Megan.

"I'm not letting you go inside by yourself."

"I probably won't go inside at all," I said. "But if I do, hold the door open."

"Mommy wasn't born in a barn," Devin said.

"Today, we're all going to act like we were, okay?" I said in my day camp counselor voice. "I'm going to pretend I'm a horse. What are you going to be?"

They were listing off farm animal names when the

door swung open, revealing a very sweaty and out of breath Zen.

"What are you doing here?" I asked.

"I live here," he said, stepping outside and closing the door behind him. "What are you doing here?"

My thoughts went back to when Scott had his naked butt pressed against the window and had seen Zen. A shiver ran down my spine. Bernadette's room overlooked the back of the hotel—where we'd found the ear.

"I—uh—came to check on everyone," I said, trying to keep my voice neutral. "I wanted to make sure the people in the cabins were safe."

"And you brought your sister and her kids too?" Zen pulled his long jacket tight around him.

"The kids needed the fresh air," Megan said. "They were going stir crazy inside."

"I don't know how any kid could go stir crazy in that lodge," he said. "It's a kid's dream."

He seemed in awe of it.

"Did you whack off the lady's ear?" Devin asked.

Megan and I whipped around as Alex clapped a hand over Devin's mouth.

"I didn't whack off anything to do with a lady." Zen chuckled.

I turned back around to see Zen still smiling at his own joke. "Why would a child ask something like that?"

"Have you seen Eloise?" I asked.

"Not since yesterday when she tried to ruin your rehearsal dinner. I assumed after that big fight that she'd be on the first snowmobile out of here."

"Apparently, fighting with her fiancé wasn't enough to

get her to leave," I said. "Nor was getting rejected by Garrett when she kissed him."

"Not the fight with Nathan—wait—she kissed Garrett?" Zen gasped. "Oh, honey. I'm so sorry. But Garrett rejected her. So that's good. I had no idea she would be such a problem. A bridezilla, yes. A home-wrecker? No—."

"Wait," I said, stopping him. "What do you mean the fight wasn't with Nathan?"

"Well, she did fight with Nathan outside your dining room. But then—about an hour later—I heard her fighting with someone else."

"Who?" I asked.

"A woman," Zen said. "At least I think it was a woman. The voice sounded feminine, but it could have just been a feminine male or a younger male. But she probably wouldn't have been fighting like this with a younger male. So it had to be a—"

"Could you tell what they were arguing about?" I asked.

"I think it had to do with Nathan and Garrett. The other person kept saying something about the plan and how stupid it was, but Eloise wasn't having it at first. Then it seemed like she was going to just give up and go home. But I guess she didn't."

I looked Zen up and down. Usually, he was the stan-dard of clean. Perfectly shaven, hair slicked back, and spot-less fingernails. But though his hair and facial hair were on point, his fingernails were nowhere near spotless. It looked like he had dirt—or something else—underneath them.

"What were you doing before you opened the door?" I asked.

"Exercising," he said, his gaze darting from me to his door and back again.

"What kind of exercise?" I asked.

"I don't mean to be rude, but that's none of your business." Zen pulled his jacket tighter around him.

"Can I come in and see your cabin?" I asked.

His eyes widened, and his head moved back on his neck, leaving him with a slight double chin. "Absolutely not. I know it may seem like we've become friends, but I promise you I'm only friendly because of the job."

"This isn't a friendly visit," I said. "I think something has happened to Eloise. I'm checking every cabin and room for evidence."

"You think I cut off Eloise's ear?" Zen laughed.

"I'm checking everyone," I said. "You were not specifically on my list."

"Last I knew, you weren't a police officer." Zen sneered at me. "And I don't think soon-to-be ex-park rangers have much authority in the way of looking into crimes."

His words stung. "Do you have something to hide?"

His gaze darted again. "No."

"Because you seem pretty shifty to me." I took a step toward him. "How do I know you weren't trying to clean up a crime scene before I got here? Huh?" I leaned in closer and lowered my voice so the boys couldn't hear me. "Maybe there's a dead body in your living room."

Zen had nowhere to go. He pushed up against his front door. "I most certainly do not have a dead body in my living room."

"Oh no," Devin said from behind me.

I turned to look at him. "What's wrong?"

"I have to piss," Devin said.

The three older boys laughed.

Megan gasped. "You do not say that word, young man."

But Devin held onto his crotch and jumped around on his tiny snowshoes. "I'm going to piss in my pants."

Now the boys were doubled over in laughter.

"Devin!" Megan turned to me. "I'll take him back to the lodge."

"No!" Devin screamed. "I won't make it!"

"Can we use your bathroom?" I asked Zen.

"Can't he just go outside?" Zen looked at the little boy, grabbing himself for dear life. "I'm sorry, but—"

"PAW-EESE! I can't piss outside. It's too cold. My piss will freeze." Devin's enormous eyes filled with tears. "If I piss my pants, my daddy will take away all my dinos."

"Stop saying piss, or I'll take your dinos!" Megan shouted. "Whatever dinos you're talking about. They're gone if you don't stop cursing."

"Just let us in," I said. "I won't snoop. He has to pee."

Zen looked at Devin. "Only him."

"Nope," Megan said. "No way. Either Rylie goes, or I go with him."

"Fine," Zen said. "You go. Rylie stays outside."

As Megan and Devin passed by me, I whispered, "Be careful and keep your eyes open."

"The bathroom down here is broken," Zen said, only opening the door wide enough to reveal a set of stairs that led up to a loft. "Use the one upstairs."

They didn't even bother taking off their snowshoes. Megan gathered up her little boy and hauled him up the stairs as he still held himself.

Zen stood in the doorway, his eyes never leaving the loft.

I tried to see past him. What was he hiding? Why wouldn't he let us in?

He didn't seem to like Eloise much, but I didn't think he had it in him to kill her. He was so into his peace, love, save the whales lifestyle, I couldn't imagine him trying to harm anyone. Though, I was starting to think his peace, love, save the whales lifestyle was a bit of a farce.

At the bottom of the stairs was something that resembled blood, but I couldn't be sure. Maybe it was dirt. Maybe he had an indoor garden, and that's why there was dirt under his nails. Maybe he had an illegal pot-growing operation.

Or maybe he killed her.

Megan and Devin hobbled back down the stairs, their steps awkward in the snowshoes.

"Don't fall," Zen said.

Once they were back outside, Zen slammed the door on us, clicking several locks into place.

"Guess what I saw," Devin said.

18

"What?" I looked at Megan, who shrugged. "What'd you see, buddy?"

"That man had a bunch of humongous dinos," Devin said. "Do you think I could get a dino?"

"I thought you said your dad takes your dinos away if you peed in your pants," I said.

"I know I'm not supposed to, but I lied," Devin said.

"You lied?" Megan asked, bending down to get eye level with him. "Why?"

"You wanted to go inside, and the silly dino man was being an assho—"

"Stop. Cussing!" Megan said.

"Sorry," he said. "He prolly just didn't want you to play with his dinos while they were eating."

"His dinos were eating?" I asked, looking at Megan for help. My nephews were known for their big imaginations.

"Meat chunks like the ones daddy makes with the spicy sauce." He laughed.

"Did the dinos move?" Megan asked him.

He looked at her as if she was stupid. "You have to move to eat, Mommy."

"Alex, can you come over here for a minute, please?" Megan asked.

Alex left the massive snow wrestling match to the two middle brothers. "Yeah?"

"What is he talking about when he says dinos?" Megan asked.

"Lizards," Alex said. "Like the ones on that show he likes to watch."

"You want me to buy you a lizard?" Megan asked.

Before he could answer, I knelt next to Devin and asked, "How did you know to say something about dinos?"

"He was wearing dino slippers," Devin said. "And Daddy told me if he got pulled over to tell the cop that I needed to pi—"

Megan gave him her scariest mom look.

"Pee," he corrected. "And I thinked it could work now too."

I pulled him into a big hug and kissed his cheeks as he giggled. "You're such a smart boy."

"Can I go get Chase now?" he asked.

"Go ahead," Megan said.

We stood and looked at each other.

"You don't think he's feeding parts of Eloise to his lizards, do you?" Megan asked with a shudder.

"There's only one way to find out," I said.

"He's not going to let you in."

"Then I'll crawl up on the roof and look myself."

"Isn't that illegal?"

"I'm pretty sure it is," I said. "But who's going to arrest me?"

"What if he did kill her?" Megan said. "It's not like you can arrest him. I know you don't like hearing this, but you're not a cop."

"I don't need to arrest him," I said. "I'm just going to sneak in and see what's going on. Take some pictures of evidence and get out. He's not going anywhere, and when the police can get back here, they can arrest him."

"What happens between now and then?" Megan asked.

"We'll keep an eye on him," I said. "Heck, I could stay in the cabin right over there and watch his every move."

"That doesn't sound terribly safe," Megan said. "What if the snow comes in harder tonight like they say it's supposed to? You might not be able to get out."

"We'll cross that bridge when we get to it," I said. "For now, I'm getting on that roof."

Megan headed out to play with the kids around the corner in case Zen peeked out the window. I took off my snowshoes and made a plan for how to get on the roof. Because the snow had drifted in the back, it was relatively easy getting up. Now, I just needed to find a window that was unlocked.

I wasn't so lucky.

All of the windows were shut tight with drapes pulled across them. My plans were unraveling.

It would only make sense that Zen would be the one who killed Eloise. He probably knew all about the cameras and how to turn them off. He likely had a master key card to access any of the rooms whenever he wanted to. Eloise was small enough even a scrawny guy like Zen would be able to carry her. Though, I wasn't sure how he did it without getting blood anywhere in the hall, down the stairs, or in the elevator.

I sat on the roof and thought for a minute. One little peek was all I needed.

Gritting my teeth, I removed a glove and applied my pretty manicured fingernails to the window. The sound was so horrible and loud when I pulled down on the glass, I heard Megan screech in the distance, "What was that?"

I ducked down beneath the windowsill, hoping Zen would walk upstairs to investigate instead of going outside. Since he was wearing slippers when he came to the door, I didn't think that would be too big an issue.

A moment later, the window opened, and Zen stuck his head out. If he looked directly down, he'd see me.

I flattened myself as much as I could against the siding, trying with everything in me not to breathe.

After a few seconds, I thought I was in the clear until I felt something grab the top of my beanie hat and a clump of my hair.

"I didn't want to have to do this," Zen said. "I know you're an important client. But you can't be sneaking around on people's roofs. And I take my privacy very seriously."

He yanked, trying to pull me inside.

"Let go of my hair," I said, trying not to scream. The last thing I needed was Megan or the boys rushing in and putting themselves in danger, too.

"You had your chance to walk away," Zen said. "Now, you're at my mercy. You wanted inside so badly, well, come on in."

I held onto his arms, trying to keep my hair from being ripped out of my scalp. I'd already had an injury when trying on wedding dresses, and my hair hadn't completely grown back in from that. One more hair issue and I wouldn't be able to cover it for the wedding.

"I'm sorry," I said. "I'm just trying to get justice for Eloise."

"I already told you, I didn't hurt Eloise."

"Then what are you hiding?"

"Let's go inside and see, shall we?" He yanked harder, but at that same moment, I pulled my head forward.

He fell backward into the upper-level bedroom, and I tumbled down the roof, landing flat on my back in the snow. While heavy wet snow was great for snowshoeing, it was like landing on concrete. All the air in my lungs had been forcibly removed, my ribs felt like they were fractured, and my head was pounding.

"You pushed her off the roof," Megan shouted at who I guessed was Zen.

"I didn't push her," Zen shouted back.

Tiny stars sprinkled my vision.

"I help you, Auntie," Devin said, rushing to my side.

"Don't move her," Bryce said. "You'll make her paralyzed."

I tried to suck in some air, but my lungs wouldn't expand.

"But we're superheroes," Devin said. "We save the day."

"What were you doing on my roof?" Zen asked, coming to stand over me.

I could hardly breathe, let alone speak.

"Leave her alone, lizard-man," Alex said, putting himself between Zen and me. He was almost as tall as Zen and probably weighed the same.

"Lizard-man?" Zen gasped. "What do you mean by that?"

"I saw your dinos," Devin said. "They were eating yucky stuff."

Zen paled.

I wiggled my fingers and toes. At least, I thought I was wiggling them.

"Rylie," Megan's voice sounded scared. "I need you to be okay right now."

I pushed up onto my elbows and took a hesitantly deep breath. "I think I'm okay. What's wrong, Meg?" My voice was strained, but the more I spoke and breathed, the better I felt. The stars in my vision started to dwindle.

Megan held out a hand for me, but it was so shaky, I worried she'd drop me on my back again. I declined and slowly pushed my way to a stand. Snow soaked my entire backside, and when I looked back at where I landed, there were specks of blood by my head. I reached up with my ungloved hand to find my fingers came back covered with blood.

"You ripped out my hair," I said.

"I didn't mean to," Zen said but kept his focus on Megan. "You were on my roof."

"Stay right there," Megan said. "You're under citizen's arrest or whatever."

"What? Why?" Zen took a step toward Megan, but Alex grabbed him by the hand and twisted in a way that sent Zen to his knees.

"My mother told you to stay where you were," Alex said, his voice low and threatening. Sometimes I forgot he wasn't a little boy anymore.

Megan walked off in the direction of the cabin. I followed.

"Tell him to let me go," Zen cried out.

"Don't hurt him too much," I said back to Alex.

Alex just gave me a mischievous grin.

"I came inside when he went to find you," Megan said, her voice shaky. "I probably shouldn't have, but I wanted to see what he was hiding."

"And?" I asked.

She motioned to the room when we walked inside. "Looks like we found our guy."

19

The scene in front of me was nothing short of gruesome. A tarp was spread on the kitchen floor with pieces of meat laid out like they were about to be photographed. Blood pooled beneath each piece.

"Where's the rest of her?" I swallowed. I didn't want to think about what the rest of her would look like.

"I think it's behind that door," Megan said. She was keeping her composure much better than I would have expected. "But it's locked."

Tiny trails of blood led from the tarp to the door. "It looks like it leads to a basement." I shivered. "I think we'll let the police handle that once we can get in touch with them."

"Good answer," Megan said as she marched to the door. "Are you coming?"

I glanced down at something shiny on the carpet. When I bent down to pick it up, my world spun. Whether it was because the shiny thing on the carpet was the earring matching the one in an ear currently in my pocket for safe-keeping, or because I'd just fallen from a roof, I didn't know.

I pulled out my phone to take a picture of the earring, yanked the hair tie out of what was left of my hair, and put it on the carpet around the earring as a sort of marker.

With one last look at the crime scene, I walked outside, locking the door behind me. Now all I needed to do was keep Zen somewhere until we could get in touch with the police.

"Alex, will you please take our friend Zen back to the lodge and ask Garrett and Cedric to make sure he doesn't go anywhere?" I asked.

He gave me a single nod, pride written all over his face.

"What?" Zen shouted. "Why?"

"I think you know why," I said.

He dropped his head to the ground, looking ashamed.

"Devin, Chase, and Bryce, you better go too for back-up." I winked at Alex, and he gave me a knowing smile.

"What else did you find in there?" Megan asked when the boys were out of earshot.

"The other earring," I said. "It was on the carpet."

She wrapped her arms around her chest as if trying to give herself a comforting hug. "I never would have thought. I guess it's a good thing you weren't a bridezilla."

"Garrett is going to be devastated," I said. "Not that we had much hope that she was still ali—"

The sight of someone darting from behind Zen's cabin headed for the trees stopped me mid-sentence.

"Who is that?" I asked. I'd specifically told everyone to stay with at least one other person.

"I don't think I've seen her before," Megan said, squinting to get a better look.

The woman was agile on her feet, even in the snow, had cropped white hair under a black beanie, and wore all black.

"Do you think she—"

I didn't hear the rest of Megan's comment before I started chasing after her.

When she saw me, she picked up speed.

If she made it to the trees, I'd probably lose her, as she was still quite far ahead of me.

"Stop," I said. "What were you doing behind Zen's cabin?"

She didn't stop. She didn't turn back to look at me.

All I could see was her white hair against all that black as she disappeared into the trees.

"Dammit," I hissed.

I stood there for a moment until the pain overwhelmed me. The stars were back in my vision. I needed to get back inside.

Megan and I walked back to the lodge where—once inside —we found a sobbing Zen. Cedric, Garrett, and all four of Megan's boys stared at him as if they had no idea what to do.

"He's been like this since he got here," Garrett said when he saw me. "What happened out there?"

I pulled him aside. "I think Eloise is dead."

Garrett sucked in a ragged breath, then nodded once. "Did you find . . . something?"

"Do you want me to tell you, or would you rather not know?" I asked.

Garrett thought about this for a minute. "I think I'd rather not know." We stood in silence for a couple of seconds before Garrett cleared his throat and turned to me. "You think Zen did it?"

"Right now, yes," I said. "Megan and I found evidence in his apartment that suggested as much."

Garrett sucked in a breath, turned away from me, and marched over to Zen, picking him up by his jacket collar. "Why did you do it?"

I rushed over. "Garrett, stop."

"I'm sorry," Zen said. "I'm so ashamed of myself. I don't know what came over me. It won't happen again."

Garrett's face was bright red. He looked like he wanted to strangle Zen.

"Put him down," I said.

Garrett finally did, shoving a sobbing Zen back onto the couch.

I followed as Garrett walked away. "The police will handle it," I said to his back. "Right now, we just need to make sure he doesn't hurt anyone else."

Garrett didn't turn back and look at me.

"I'm really sorry about your friend," I said. "I know how I'd feel if something happened to Luke."

This stopped Garrett in his tracks.

He turned to look at me, his face streaked with tears.

At first, I thought he might have been offended by my statement, but when he gathered me up in his arms, I realized I had nothing to worry about. *Love is not easily provoked.* Garrett wins the award for best future husband again.

"Thank you for understanding," he said. "You're going to be the best wife."

Love does not seek its own. Guilt settled into my gut that I wasn't as broken up about Eloise's death as I should have been. Especially when she was someone important to Garrett. I hugged him tighter. I'd learn to be a good wife. After everything I put him through, I owed him that much.

20

Everyone returned before dark, meeting in the den. The limited kitchen staff set up a nice little buffet of soups, chilis, and bread bowls. It was the perfect comfort meal. I insisted everyone enjoy their food before we went over our findings for the day.

Cedric had taken Zen to an open meeting room off the beaten path, so it wasn't obvious that we'd found anything.

Once the room was quiet—bellies full—we started going around the room with anything and everything we found odd about the day.

Scott and Bernadette had gone through five different cabins—only one—finding nothing but a newlywed couple who seemed more than a bit put out to have had to leave their bed.

If only I hadn't gotten twisted up in yet another murder investigation. I could just imagine spending the duration of the snowstorm enjoying the company of my fiancé. I peeked over at him, but by the look on his face, he didn't seem to be thinking the same thing.

He'd barely spoken since his altercation with Zen. Bernadette kept shooting him looks, trying to figure out what was going on with him, but he was oblivious.

Mom and Dad had gone to the event center but had found nothing of interest.

Tom and Hugo were the only ones who found something vaguely of interest.

"When we were coming back from the cabin on the north side of the property," Tom said. "We saw a woman sneaking around in the trees."

"We might not have seen her if it hadn't been for her white hair," Hugo added.

I nodded. "I saw the same woman. I tried to run after her, but after nearly freezing to death last night and falling off the roof this afternoon, my body just wasn't in the mood to react very quickly. She got away."

"Did anyone else see someone who matches that description?" Megan asked.

No one had.

"All right," I said. "I suppose that leaves us."

Megan nodded. We'd intentionally left the boys upstairs with the nanny, so they wouldn't interject their comments. Though I was certain their comments would be nothing short of adorable, this was not the time for cute. This was the moment I revealed to everyone that a woman was dead and that we'd found her killer.

"Do you want me to tell them?" Megan asked when I said nothing for a few minutes.

"No," Garrett said. "Rylie should."

I wasn't sure why he wanted me to, but I had planned on it, anyway. "As you all remember, we found the ear with the earring near the snowshoe hut."

Nods came from around the room.

"We have reason to believe Eloise has passed away," I said.

Bernadette stood. "Why didn't you say that to begin with?"

"I wanted everyone to have the opportunity to get some food," I said. "I didn't think with this news anyone would end up being very hungry."

"How can you be sure she's dead?" Bernadette asked.

"For now, I won't disclose my reasoning," I said. "The police will probably be able to get here tomorrow or the next day. Once they take over the scene, they can release whatever information they deem relevant."

Megan nodded.

Bernadette looked furious. "This is my daughter." She took a step toward me. "You'll tell me right now why you think she's dead."

"I also think we caught the killer," I said.

Bernadette's eyes widened. "What? Who?" She glanced around the room. "Nathan? Is that why he's been conveniently missing since this morning?"

Now that she mentioned it, I realized he had been missing.

"It's not Nathan," I said. "Though, we should probably find him and break the news to him gently."

"If it's not Nathan, then who did it?" Bernadette asked.

"I believe Zen—the wedding planner—killed your

daughter." I held my composure. It would do no good for me to lose it right now.

"The skinny little vegan?" Bernadette asked. "There's no way."

"I assure you, I don't make accusations lightly." *Anymore*, I thought to myself. I'd accused people way too quickly in the past. But I'd gotten better at investigation as time had gone on.

"What's his motive?" Bernadette asked.

"We haven't been able to glean anything from him yet," Garrett said. "He's spent most of his time sobbing."

Bernadette threw her hands in the air. "So that's it? You're just going to let him roam around sobbing after he killed my daughter?"

"He's being watched," Garrett said.

"And, as I said before," I added. "The police will take everything over when they can get here. Tonight, all we can do is try to get some rest. We've all had a big day with lots of stress and emotion. You were wonderful. All of you. Thank you so much for your help."

With that, I stood up and began to walk out of the den.

"Where are you going?" Bernadette asked.

"There's nothing else for me to do right now," I said. "We caught the killer. The evidence overwhelmingly points to Zen. I'm so sorry about your loss, but I'm exhausted. I fell off a roof, lost part of my scalp, and can barely hold myself upright."

"You never cared about Eloise," Bernadette said. "You're probably happy she's dead."

"I didn't *know* Eloise existed until yesterday," I said.

"And I'm not happy she's dead. In fact, I wish she was still alive. For your sake. For Garrett's sake."

"Why?" Bernadette spat. "Now, you're the winner."

"Winner?" I asked. "Pretty sure I was the winner before she died."

Bernadette tipped her head back. "Ha! You think you were. But my girl had you beat. If she had had more time with Garrett before someone offed her, she would have easily won." Bernadette narrowed her eyes at me. "Where were you the night she went missing?"

"I was at the pool," I said. "We've already been over this."

"Can anyone corroborate your story?"

"Scott was there," I said.

Scott nodded in agreement but stopped when Bernadette looked over at him.

"You and Zen seemed awfully buddy-buddy before all of this," Bernadette said. "Maybe you helped him kill her, and now you're trying to pin everything on him."

"Fine," I said. "Then have the police talk to me when they get here. I swear, I won't leave my room. Do you want to escort me there?"

"Yes," she said.

I grumbled but didn't have the energy to argue with her.

We got in the elevator, and she pushed the button to my floor. Neither of us spoke. There was nothing left to say. All I wanted was a soft pillow and a blanket or two.

And Fizzy.

My eyes glazed over with tears. I missed my pooch.

When the elevator doors opened, I marched down the

hallway past Bernadette, pulled out my key card, and walked into the room.

I was flopping down onto the bed when I heard a gasp and then a scream. It was then I realized I hadn't heard the door click into place.

When Bernadette emerged from the bathroom holding a bloody knife, I saw my life flash before my eyes.

21

My feet were under me within seconds.

"Put the knife down," I said, holding my hands out in front of me. I'd taken knife defense training as a park ranger, but knives freaked me out. Probably more than guns. Knives were a multi-directional weapon, whereas guns—when shot—only had one trajectory.

"You killed her," Bernadette said. "This is proof right here."

"I don't know how that got in my room," I said. "Why would I have left the bloody knife just lying around for anyone to see it?"

"You probably didn't think anyone would come in here after we searched the place." Bernadette took a step toward me, her mouth puckered in anger, knife pointed at me. "You've been a part of so many investigations—Eloise sends me news links about you all the time. I bet you know exactly how to make yourself look innocent, don't you?"

"I've never seen someone get away with murder," I said. "I know it happens, but I don't know how to make it happen."

"You think I'm that stupid?" Bernadette took another step toward me. "What do you think they'll think when everyone finds out you had the murder weapon in your hotel room this entire time and didn't care to mention it to anyone?"

"If it had been in my hotel room the entire time, wouldn't someone have found it when rifling through my stuff? And since they didn't find it, why would I have gotten it out to leave it out in plain view?" I shook my head. "Also, what about the knife sticking out of Garrett's door with Eloise's engagement ring on it?"

"Maybe you worked with someone else to kill her," Bernadette said. "Maybe your sister helped. Maybe there were two knives."

"Megan didn't do anything," I said. "Nor did I. Now, put the knife down."

This woman was tiny but fierce. And I was running out of room behind me. My only options would be to fight or try to launch myself over the bed and make it to the door.

"I'm not putting it down," she said. "I'm going to do to you what you did to my daughter."

"You don't even know what happened to her," I said.

"I know there was a lot of blood. And I know they'll think I acted in self-defense. Which this basically is, if you think about it. I'm defending the person I love most in the world. I'm just slightly late."

She lunged, and I spun away from the knife blade. When she lunged again, I was already on the bed.

I would have made it to the door if my foot hadn't gotten tangled in the sheets, sending me to the floor flat on my face.

Bernadette laughed. "You shouldn't have messed with us."

I rolled over to see her with the knife raised over her head, her entire body shaking with rage.

With one fluid motion, she brought the knife down.

I rolled again, grabbing her ankle and pulling as hard as I could.

Bernadette went down with a thud, the knife slicing through the back of my shirt and into my skin.

We both screamed in pain.

I yanked the knife out of her hand as we both struggled to come to a stand.

Her gaze darted from me to the door, and then she fell to the ground covering her head, screaming, "Please, don't kill me like you killed Eloise!"

The dramatics were too much for the situation.

When I turned to look behind me at the door, I realized why.

Garrett stood in the doorway with a look of pure panic on his face.

2 2

I held my hands up in the air. "I wasn't going to hurt her. She cut me, see?" I turned around to show him the knife wound going all the way up my back.

"I was trying to get away from her," Bernadette said, scurrying away on her knees and gripping Garrett's ankles like a child who didn't want their mother to leave them at daycare.

"She was threatening to kill me," I said.

"Then why did I find the murder weapon in your bathroom?" Bernadette asked. "Huh?"

Garrett stood staring at me. "Rylie?"

"I don't know how it got in my bathroom," I said.

"She was so threatened by Eloise that she had to kill her," Bernadette wailed.

Garrett's gaze shot to me. "Threatened? I thought you weren't the jealous type."

"I'm not," I said. "But I also didn't expect to encounter you and your ex-almost-fiancée the night before our supposed wedding kissing in a deserted hallway."

"See?" Bernadette said.

I sighed. "So I was jealous. That doesn't mean I killed her. You know me better than that, right?"

Garrett didn't seem like he knew what to think.

"Well?" Bernadette asked Garrett.

"Look," Garrett said. "I'm exhausted, just like everyone else. Why don't we sleep on it and see if things are clearer in the morning?"

"Nope," Bernadette said. "We can't just let her sleep."

Little did she know, they wouldn't have much of a choice soon. As the adrenaline subsided in my body for the thousandth time today, I felt heavy, like I wouldn't be able to hold myself up much longer.

I sat on the bed. "If you're so worried, stay here tonight."

"I'm not staying in your room. You'll probably kill me too," Bernadette said.

"Not you," I said through a yawn. "Garrett."

Garrett nodded. "Okay."

Bernadette looked at the two of us and then got to her feet. "I'll be back first thing in the morning with the police."

"I look forward to it," I said as she walked out the door.

Garrett picked up the knife with a washcloth and put it back in the bathroom, then climbed into the other queen bed without a single word.

"You can sleep over here," I said.

But he didn't reply, just stared at the wall.

I laid down, remembering the gash on my back. When I sat back up, blood had stained the bedsheets.

If I hadn't been so tired, I might have done something about it, but I didn't even have it in me to cry about my fiancé refusing to speak to me. Or sleep in the same bed as me.

Bernadette didn't show up at my room first thing the next morning. In fact, I didn't see her until we were all downstairs for breakfast.

The mood was somber. Garrett still hadn't spoken to me other than the five words about whether I wanted to shower before going down to breakfast.

The water had burned the cut on my back and the part of my scalp that had been torn off. When I looked closer, neither of the wounds were as bad as I feared, though the back one would probably leave a faint scar.

I thought about my wedding dress. Would I still be able to wear my hair up? Or would I need to leave it down?

Across the room, Garrett watched me as he nibbled on his bacon. Would there even still be a wedding? I wanted to march right up to him and give him all sorts of pieces of my mind, but before I could, Bernadette burst through the door.

"He's dead," she cried out.

I stood to my feet, leaving the half-eaten plate of food on the table. "Who's dead?"

"I went to check on him because—well—I was mad," Bernadette said, her words coming out in bursts. "He didn't even care that she was dead. Didn't help search for her. Nothing. So, I went to his room. But when I opened the door, he was face down on the bed with a knife in his back."

"Nathan?" I asked. "Nathan is dead?"

"That's what I've been trying to tell you," Bernadette said. "Zen must have gotten out of his room and killed Nathan too."

I glanced at Garrett, who was pulling out his phone, probably to check for service.

"Let's go up there and see, shall we?" I asked.

The rest of the people in the room watched as we walked out. Garrett stood and followed, though, whether he was coming to see what had happened or to protect one of us from the other, I wasn't certain.

"How did you get into her room?" I asked.

She pulled out a keycard. "She gave me a copy, just in case I needed to get inside."

"Do you know if she gave anyone else a copy?" I asked.

"Maybe that *sister* of hers." Bernadette used her fingers to do air quotes when she said the word sister.

"Have you seen Courtney?" Garrett asked, his voice surprising both of us.

"No," Bernadette said.

"Not at all since you've been here?" I asked.

She shook her head. "No desire to. As I said, she's not my daughter."

I wanted to wring this woman's neck. Why Garrett would have ever wanted to be part of her family was beyond me. Granted, his family had some crazy in it, too.

Love is not arrogant.

I was being arrogant, thinking my family was better than both of theirs.

Ugh. I just couldn't help myself, could I?

The elevator door slid open, revealing the hallway that led to Nathan and Eloise's room.

Bernadette slid her key card in, and the light on the reader turned green. With a click and a turn of the handle, we were in.

"Uh," Garrett said, surveying the room. "I thought you said there was a body."

"Not again," I muttered.

There was a lot of blood, but no body.

"He was here less than five minutes ago," Bernadette said. "I saw him."

"Did you take a picture for evidence or anything?" I asked, looking around. "Maybe one of the knife sticking out of his back?"

As if on cue, my back began to burn from my own knife wound. At least I was still alive.

"I-I didn't think to," Bernadette said. "I thought I'd come get you, and you could do all that."

"I guess you were unsuccessful in getting the police to come first thing this morning to arrest me?" I picked up a short white hair with my gloved hand and examined it.

"The phones are still not working. I tried the moment I woke up." Bernadette scowled at me, then turned to Garrett. "Was she with you the entire morning?"

"That's enough," Garrett said. "Stop accusing Rylie of murdering people she barely knew. She had no reason to murder Eloise. Eloise kissed me, and Rylie and I discussed it. She was fine. We were going to get married. And why in the world would she kill Nathan?"

Bernadette looked like she'd been slapped in the face.

And I felt like I had, too. Had he said we *were* going to get married? As in past tense? As in we weren't anymore?

I didn't glance up at him for fear that my face would give away my emotions.

"Please apologize to Rylie," Garrett said.

Bernadette looked down at her feet.

"Bernadette?" Garret's tone was the same one a mother would use on the playground to make her child apologize for throwing sand at another child.

"Fine," Bernadette finally said. "I'm sorry. But I'm not lying. I swear there was another body."

"Then we need to talk to Zen." I pulled a mini muffin out of my pocket, took it out of its zip-top bag, and placed the hair inside. "Maybe he wasn't working alone. And the real target was to kill both of them in the first place." I shoved the muffin into my mouth.

"That's so ladylike," Bernadette said.

I rolled my eyes but then instantly worried that maybe Garrett wanted someone more ladylike. I stood straighter and brushed the crumbs from my lips. "Sorry."

The walk to where we had kept Zen was silent. Even though Garrett had stood up for me, he didn't put his arm around me or hold my hand like normal.

I desperately wanted to ask him about the wedding but didn't need Bernadette to hear our conversation. Especially when she seemed bound and determined to break us up, even though her daughter was gone and wouldn't be able to marry him, anyway.

Cedric opened the door, looking exhausted. "Shift change?"

"Almost," Garrett said, taking the lead.

"Was Zen here all night and all morning?" I asked.

Cedric nodded. "He cried himself to sleep last night and hasn't woken up since."

The bed had a human-shaped lump under the covers and Zen's hair poking out over the top.

"Did you fall asleep at all? Is there any way Zen could have left this room?" I asked.

Cedric yawned. "I wish I had. Then I wouldn't be so dang tired. But—no—I watched him all night. Didn't even use the bathroom."

I half expected to see pillows and a strategically placed wig when Garrett pulled back the covers—that would be my luck—but Zen was there. Thankfully.

"Hey, that's not nice," Zen said.

"Get up," Garrett said.

"Am I finished?" Cedric asked.

I nodded. Garrett seemed to have the bodyguarding under control.

"Dude, let go," Zen said. "Are the cops here?"

"Did you leave this room last night or this morning?" Garrett asked.

Zen rolled over. "I'm not one to take my own life into my hands. If I'd have tried to leave, the black hulk would have killed me."

"Were you working with anyone to kill Eloise?" I asked. "If so, they're out there killing people still."

He turned back over and looked at me. His eyes were puffy like he'd been crying all night. "I didn't kill anyone. I don't know how many times I have to tell you that."

"Then why is there blood all over your cabin?" I asked.

Zen paled and rolled back over. "That's none of your business."

I yanked Zen back over by his arm. "Listen here. I have had about enough of your whiny ass throwing a temper tantrum after what I found in your cabin. Chopped up pieces of meat on a tarp. Blood trickling to a locked basement. And one of Eloise's earrings—the same one as we found in her chopped-off ear."

Zen's eyes widened. "You found her earring in my cabin?"

I crossed my arms over my chest and glared down at him. "Don't play dumb with me. It's only a matter of time before the police get into that basement, and then everything's over for you."

"You have it all wrong," Zen sat up in his bed. "There's no way Eloise's earring could have been in my house. She's never been inside my house. Someone has to be setting me up."

"What about all the—uh—other stuff?" Garrett asked.

I glanced up at him to find his face white as the sheets Zen was tangled up in. I'd forgotten he hadn't wanted to hear about what was in Zen's cabin. And I'd just blabbed it all.

"That's . . ." Zen was hiding something, but I was starting to think it wasn't about Eloise. "It's elk meat." His voice came out in a whisper so low I almost didn't hear him.

"Elk meat?" I asked.

"I'm so ashamed," Zen said. "I killed it."

"The elk?" I asked.

"For my lizards. I was worried they'd starve," Zen said. "I grew up hunting with my father but changed my ways in college. All those majestic animals murdered for disgusting humans to eat. I became a vegan. It was better for me. Less guilt. But the snowstorm caught me off-guard. The shipment for my lizards was supposed to come this weekend. I'd procrastinated, and they were down to their last meal. So, I took the gun I kept locked up in the basement for emergencies and did what I said I'd never do again."

"You killed an elk," Garrett said.

"Not just an elk," Zen said. "A little elk."

"A baby?" I gasped.

"Not a baby," Zen said, horrified. "It was probably at least a teenager. But it was scrawny. I told myself I was doing it a favor. That it wouldn't live through the winter. But in reality, I knew I had to go for a little one or else I'd never get it back to my cabin with these scrawny vegan arms." He pushed a finger into his squishy bicep. "I didn't want to make a mess, so I brought out a tarp and started cleaning the meat like I'd learned as a child."

Garrett looked at me. "Do you hunt?"

I shook my head. "You?"

"No," he said. "I guess our kids won't hunt either, then."

Our kids? My heart warmed. Apparently, he did still want to marry me.

I turned back to Zen. "If we go back to your cabin and into the basement, we'll find the remains of an elk, not a human, right?"

"The elk is what I was lugging down the stairs when you knocked. If you find the remains of a human, it'll only be proof that someone is trying to set me up." Zen huffed. "That's the only way that earring could have gotten there."

"Where's the key for the basement door?" I asked.

"In the cabinet under the main floor bathroom sink," Zen said. "Go ahead and look. And when you don't find anything, will you let me go?"

"We'll see," Garrett said, then turned to me. "Are you going to go check it out?"

"I think I should," I said. "There's no use holding an innocent man captive."

Garrett grabbed my hand. "I'm so sorry I was cold to you last night. I didn't know what to think, and I was so tired, and—with the whole Eloise thing—I'm just a mess."

"It's okay," I said. "Do you still want to marry me?"

"Just as soon as I possibly can." Garrett pulled me close to him and kissed me gently on the lips. "This changes nothing between us. Eloise is my past. Am I sad she's gone? Definitely. But I haven't spoken with her since we broke up. I guess the bigger question is, do you still want to marry me after I didn't immediately take your side last night?"

I thought about it for a minute—*love does not hold grudges*—then said, "Yes, of course, I do."

He hugged me tightly. "When you go to his cabin, can you take someone with you? If he didn't hurt anyone, there's still a killer out there. I wouldn't forgive myself if you were the next victim."

"I'll see if Megan can go with me," I said.

"Will you check on my lizards too?" Zen asked. "Just make sure they're okay."

"Sure," I said.

Garrett kissed me one more time before I walked out of the room.

I had every intention of getting Megan, but no one was in her room, and when I went back down to breakfast, everyone had left.

I figured it wouldn't take long to determine whether Zen was telling the truth, so I headed outside in the blistering wind back to his cabin.

Where Garrett and Cedric had shoveled, there was now a fresh drift, which made it challenging to get to the supply hut. Once I got my snowshoes on, it was only a few minutes before I made it to Zen's cabin. I took a deep breath before trying to turn the handle, only to remember I'd locked the door the day before.

I circled to the back of the cabin, but that door was locked, too. I groaned in frustration.

It wasn't until I was about to break a window, I remembered the window Zen had tried to pull me into.

It was still open.

My insides tightened. I didn't know much about lizards, but I knew they didn't do well in the cold.

I took off my snowshoes and climbed on the roof for the second time in twenty-four hours. This time was even easier than the first because of the extra snow, but every time my back twisted, the knife wound rubbed against my shirt, sending pain shooting through my body.

When I got to the open window, I pushed myself through, trying not to think too much about what I'd find both with the lizards and with the basement.

The room was relatively warm, considering the wind howling outside.

When I peeked into the gigantic tank, the massive lizards were still moving, just a bit more slowly than I figured they normally did. If I got the window closed and the heat back up, they'd probably be okay.

I sighed in relief. One less thing to feel guilty about.

With the window shut and the heavy curtains closed, I headed downstairs.

The living room and kitchen were exactly as we'd left them. My hair tie was still around the earring. The meat—now rotting and putrid-smelling—was still on the tarp.

I went into the bathroom—which was also covered in blood, probably because he'd gone in there to clean up before he'd answered the door—to find the key.

It was where he said it was.

When I turned it in the lock, the door opened.

It was so easy. Too easy.

Or maybe it was only easy because I was really going to find an elk downstairs and realize I'd caught the wrong person. Again. And here I was thinking I was getting better at investigation. Apparently, not. Which was fine by me. Once Garrett and I were married, and I'd officially quit my job as a ranger once and for all, I'd never have to investigate another crime again.

I flipped on the light to find a trail of blood leading down the steps. It looked like Zen had basically just thrown the elk head and carcass down the stairs, as it was lying at the bottom staring up at me with its dead beady eye.

I shivered. Not a single part of me wanted to go into that basement. But Zen could have been lying. He could have killed the elk to cover up what he'd actually done. And if I didn't investigate further and let Zen go, he could join up with his partner in crime and kill again.

Steeling myself, I started down the stairs. I didn't look at the elk. It was too sad. I'd guess Zen was going to use all the parts for something or other before I'd practically forced him to chuck it down the stairs. Now, it was probably completely ruined.

Once in the basement, I searched for a light to illuminate the space as the light from the stairs barely reached the rest of the room.

Finally, I found a pull chain connected to a single lightbulb. At the same time, my gaze landed on Nathan's body, the door at the top of the stairs slammed shut.

25

I darted away from the body and took the stairs two at a time. Sure enough, the door was locked. Who put a double-sided locking mechanism on a basement door? If only I'd pocketed the key, I'd have been able to get myself out. Unless they were keyed differently. Was that even possible?

I pressed my ear against the door, hoping to hear someone speak or footsteps or anything. But it was silent.

Maybe the door had swung shut on its own?

I shook my head. That was unlikely. All the doors and windows were closed, and there wasn't a spring or anything that would have closed the door automatically.

My mind went back to the body I'd just seen. Not the elk. The human.

Nathan.

Bernadette had been telling the truth. Well, at least the part about him being dead.

First Eloise and now Nathan?

Maybe someone had it out for the family. Maybe this had nothing to do with me after all.

I walked back down the stairs and took the time to examine the body.

He'd definitely been stabbed, though there wasn't any blood on the floor. Whatever blood had drained from him had done so somewhere else—probably in his hotel room.

His hair was matted to his face, and his skin was gray. I'd guess he'd been dead for a while.

If only we could test the blood in the kitchen and the bathroom. Though, if Zen had known Nathan's body was in his basement, he likely wouldn't have told me how to go down here.

So, if Zen didn't kill him, who did?

I considered the options.

The mysterious half-sister seemed like someone I at least needed to speak to. She could be responsible for both deaths. And if she was the one with white hair, it was almost a sure thing she had something to do with Nathan's murder.

I pulled out my phone and turned on the flashlight to check his body more closely.

Another strand of white hair was lodged in his, and when I looked more closely, I realized something on the side of his head didn't look right.

I used my gloved hand to pull his hair back off his face, revealing a missing ear.

I gasped.

The only reason we thought Eloise was dead was because we found an ear with her earring in it and the chopped-up meat that ended up being elk meat.

Could Eloise still be alive?

Did she kill Nathan to make it look like she was dead?

Or maybe someone had her alive somewhere but wanted us to think she was dead. Someone like a sister? Who might be in line for some sort of inheritance?

My heart raced. I had to get out of the basement and look at that ear.

I'd left it in the mini-fridge in a baggie in my hotel room.

I rushed back to the top of the stairs and tried the door again.

It still wouldn't budge.

"Help!" I screamed. "I'm trapped down here!"

I yelled and pounded on the door until my lungs and fists hurt.

I searched the rest of the basement for any way to get out, but the windows were high and completely covered in snow. I'd have to tunnel out, which wouldn't be safe. I could easily get buried.

Tears stung at my eyes. How did I always get myself into these predicaments? Had I not figured anything out by now?

At least Garrett knew where I was. When I didn't come back, he'd surely come looking for me. Or at least send someone to if he was still guarding Zen.

But as time went on, I realized the flaw in my plan.

Garrett had no way of communicating with anyone until they took over guarding Zen. Which meant I would likely be stuck in a basement with a dead man and a dead elk for hours.

I wasn't tired, so sleeping wasn't an option.

What I really needed to do was get my thoughts on paper.

Paper.

I needed to find paper.

I searched through Zen's basement. Surely, he had to have something down here that I could use to write on and with.

Finally, I came across a box that had half-used notebooks and pens.

I did my best not to snoop, but from the looks of things, Zen was a poet.

I flipped to a blank page and started writing down everything I knew.

Eloise may or may not be dead. If she were dead or hurt, the suspects would be Nathan, her sister, my sister . . .

The idea popped into my head, but I quickly shook it away. There was no way Megan would have hurt Eloise. Even if she thought it would help me, it just didn't make sense.

But she wasn't in her room that night.

That's why the boys had gone down to the pool.

Had I asked her what she was doing?

Other than following Garrett?

I wrote another name at the top of the page.

Nathan.

I'd think about Megan more at a later time.

Who would want Nathan dead?

Eloise? Maybe he'd hurt her, and she went after him. But then why put her own earrings in his ears? And how would tiny little Eloise get Nathan's body from his room in the hotel to Zen's basement?

She'd have to have help.

Maybe her sister helped her.

Or maybe her sister thought Nathan hurt Eloise, and she did something about it.

Frankly, Bernadette could be added to the list of suspects for Nathan.

She might have alerted us to the body to make it look like she was innocent. She did have a key to their room, after all.

And then there was Garrett. If he knew Nathan had hurt Eloise, I could only imagine what he might do.

No.

He was one of the kindest men I'd ever met. He wouldn't hurt someone.

Unless he thought they deserved it.

I glanced over and shined my light at Nathan again.

If someone had seen him hurt Eloise and they hurt him, it only made sense that they wouldn't offer information they had about Eloise because they'd instantly become a suspect.

But that would also mean Eloise would have to be dead.

Unless she was alive and hiding. And the person knew that.

My head spun. Nothing was coming together. There just weren't enough clues.

Then my light caught on Nathan's hand. Something was written on it.

I hurried over and looked more closely.

On one palm, the words Bernadette and Courtney were written in what looked like faded permanent marker.

On the other palm, he had written what looked like a code of some sort—PV222.

Or maybe it was DV222. It was hard to make out.

What did that mean?

And why did he have Bernadette and Courtney's names written on his palm?

Had he still been alive when he got to the basement and wrote the words, so we knew who killed him?

I searched the floor and under the shelves but didn't find a permanent marker anywhere.

The words were faded too, which probably meant they'd been there for at least one shower if not two.

I glanced back at my pad of paper and added the code PV222 with DV222? in parentheses next to it.

"Rylie?" A voice came from the other side of the door. It was Garrett.

"I'm in here," I said. "I got locked in."

I ripped the piece of paper off the page and shoved it into my jacket pocket before replacing the notebook and pen in the box where I'd found them.

"Do you have the key?" Garrett asked.

"No," I said. "It should be out there. I left it in the door, and the door closed on me."

"There's no key out here," Garrett said. "Someone must have locked you in."

I hadn't wanted to accept that possibility, but there was no other explanation.

"Did you find Eloise down there?" His voice was quieter with this question.

"No," I said. "But I found Nathan and the elk. They're both dead."

"But you're sure Eloise isn't down there?"

"I'm sure," I said, glancing back. "I searched the place high and low, trying to find another way out."

"The door looks pretty sturdy," Garrett said. "But I'll see if I can kick it in."

Garrett was built like a football player. If anyone could kick in the door, he could.

"Stand back," he said.

I went to the bottom of the stairs, careful not to step on the elk.

He kicked once. The sound of wood splintering was music to my ears, but the door still wasn't open.

On the second kick, the door burst from its hinges, the frame breaking under the force.

I rushed up the stairs and into Garrett's open arms.

"Why didn't you bring someone with you?" Garrett asked as he buried his face in my neck.

"I tried to find Megan, but when I couldn't, I figured I'd just make a quick trip to confirm what Zen told us."

"But you found Nathan down there?"

"Yeah," I said. "It looks like he was tortured. Or at least his ear was cut off."

"His ear?" Garrett said, glancing down the stairs and then turning away. "Maybe this is a serial killer who cuts people's ears off."

I hadn't considered that possibility.

"Or maybe someone cut his ear off and pushed her earring through it to make it look like Eloise was dead," I said. "I didn't look at the ear we found very closely to see if the ear looked masculine or feminine. If that's even a thing."

Garrett looked at me. "You think there's a possibility Eloise is still alive?"

I didn't want to get his hopes up, but I couldn't lie to him. "A slight possibility."

"Then we can still find her." He grabbed my hand and pulled me back outside.

The sun was so bright, it was hard to see without sunglasses. "If the weather stays nice, we might be able to have our wedding after all."

"I'm counting on it," Garrett said.

I found my snowshoes behind the house and put them back on.

Garrett and I quickly made our way back to the hotel, and as we walked through the doors, a woman with white hair came barreling out.

26

"Courtney?" Garrett asked, grabbing the woman by her shoulders. "Where have you been? Have you heard what's happened to El—"

"Garrett, stop," I said. "We need to talk to her and see what she knows before we give her any details."

Courtney's eyes widened. "What I know about what?"

"Come on," I said. "Let's go inside and talk."

She tried to pull away from Garrett, but he kept a firm grasp on her. "Come on, Court, don't make this any harder than it has to be."

Court? He didn't call Megan Meg. Though no one did. But that was beside the point.

Love was not jealous.

But Rylie was.

Dammit.

Courtney finally obliged and went willingly as Garrett took her to the den.

The only person in the room was the staff member cleaning up from lunch.

We sat as far from the lunch buffet as possible.

"What are you doing here?" Garrett asked.

"Eloise asked me to be here," she said. "Something about trying to break up your wedding."

Well, there it was. I guess the secret was out.

"What about Nathan?" I asked.

"Nathan was a pawn in her plan," she said. "Until he got jealous and became violent."

"What do you mean?"

"Nothing," she said. "It's nothing. I want a lawyer or something. You can't question me without my say-so. This is illegal. I'll call daddy."

"I'm not a cop," I said. "And neither is Garrett. We're just trying to find out what happened to Eloise."

"She's dead," Courtney said. "Don't you get that? He killed her."

"Who killed her?" I asked.

"Nathan," she said as if I was the dumbest person on the planet. "Who else would kill her? She was perfection."

"And how do you know he killed her?" I asked, ignoring the perfection comment and the fact that Garrett wasn't disputing it.

"I saw him carrying her bloody body into the women's locker room," she said.

"Don't you mean out of?" I asked.

She frowned. "No. Into. I thought I'd hit the gym for a quick run before bed. But when the elevator door opened, I saw him holding her and walking into the locker room."

"And you're sure she was already bloody?" I asked.

"Yes," she said. "Who are you anyway?"

"Rylie is my fiancé," Garrett said.

"You're the woman who replaced Eloise?" She let out a high-pitched laugh. "That's absurd."

"Why is that absurd?" I asked.

"Garrett could have anyone," she said. "He wouldn't choose someone so . . . homely."

Homely was not something I'd ever been called before.

"Come on, Court," Garrett said. "Be nice."

"Why? You're being an idiot." Courtney sat up straighter in her seat. "So she turned you down all those years ago. She wanted you back. She called you multiple times."

"And I told her I was with Rylie," Garrett said, reaching for my hand.

His touch wasn't all that comforting. Why hadn't he told me about her phone calls? Or about her at all?

"I love Rylie," he continued. "And we're getting married."

"It doesn't matter, anyway. Not now that Eloise is gone." Courtney's eyes glassed over with tears.

As much as I wanted to hate her, I still needed to get information out of her. Plus, I'd be incredibly heartbroken if anything happened to Megan. "What happened when you saw them go into the pool? Did you go in after them?"

"Of course I did," she said. "And I confronted him, but he threatened me with a knife. He told me she was already dead, and if I knew what was good for me, I'd get out."

"And did you?" Garrett asked.

"Like my feet were on fire," she said. "Then I saw Scott

in the hall. I told him what happened, but he thought I was joking. Bernadette believed me, though."

"Wait, you saw Bernadette and Scott?" Garrett asked.

"We went back to Bernadette's room, where she tried to calm me down." Courtney wiped a tear from her cheek. "But then you showed up with your sister, and she left."

"So she wasn't only in there with Scott, she was in there with both of you," Garrett said.

"And when she left, Scott and I went down to the pool, but Eloise was gone," Courtney said.

A commotion came from behind us as Scott and Bernadette burst into the room.

"What did she tell you?" Bernadette yelled, pointing her finger at Courtney.

"I didn't tell them—" Courtney started, but I clapped a hand over her mouth.

"Stop," I said. "Do not say another word. Any of you."

Everyone stopped. Even I was surprised by the authority in my voice.

"Garrett, stay with Courtney," I said. "I'm going to talk to these two about what Courtney just told us."

Courtney looked down at her hands in her lap.

"Come on," I said, leading Bernadette and Scott out of the den. "Let's go into the lobby."

"Can we do this somewhere a bit more private?" Bernadette asked.

"There's no one here," I said. "The lobby will be just fine."

Bernadette and I sat on the couches when we reached the lobby, but Scott didn't sit down. His eyes shifted toward the door, and before I could stop him, he bolted.

The door had apparently been shoveled out, and Scott was gone, the doors slamming closed behind him.

"That little weasel," Bernadette muttered under her breath.

"Courtney told us everything," I said. "Now, I can either tell the police that you assisted in the investigation, or I can tell them you didn't."

"I can't go to jail," she said. "I didn't kill anyone. They did. The two of them."

"Right," I said, surprised by her outburst. "Why don't you start from the beginning."

I tried to keep the shock off my face as she spoke.

"They came to my room the night you found Eloise," she said. "Courtney said she saw Nathan carrying Eloise into the locker room. She was freaking out, saying he had a knife and told her to leave because Eloise was already dead."

I nodded along with her story.

"I tried to calm her down—to get her to tell me what was going on—but then you showed up and said Eloise was missing." She shifted in her seat. "Nathan didn't even care that his fiancé was missing. He didn't look for her at all. He lied. He's the one who did something to her. But you said she was still alive when you saw her, so Scott suggested we have a chat with Nathan."

"And when did this happen?" I asked.

"Just before we all went out to search the cabins," she said. "Nathan went back to his room. He had no intention of searching for her. Because he knew what happened to her."

She took a deep breath and glanced around to make sure no one was listening.

"I thought we were just going to talk to him," Bernadette continued. "You know? Like, threaten him or something. But Scott chopped his ear off when Nathan said he didn't know where Eloise was. Then Courtney saw red and started stabbing him. I wanted to leave—I had nothing to do with all of this—but they said I'd be complicit in the crime since I didn't stop it. That I was just as guilty as they were."

I had to bite my lower lip to keep my jaw from hanging open.

"Did Nathan ever tell you what really happened to Eloise?" I asked.

"He kept saying it was her idea. She turned off the cameras and left blood on the switches to make it look like a crime. Then she took some pills to stop her heart, but he said she should have woken up," she said. "The blood wasn't real. At least, he said it wasn't. He said she was just trying to make everyone think she was gone so Garrett would re-think the wedding and choose her."

"That seems like an awfully extreme plan just to get a guy to choose you," I said.

"She was desperate," Bernadette said. "She'd tried everything else with Garrett, but he was insistent he'd already made a promise to you, and he would stick with it."

"So before they killed him, he told you Eloise should still be alive?" I asked.

"I don't think they meant to kill him," Bernadette said. "We tried to stop the bleeding, but it was too much. Then

Scott mentioned Zen didn't like Eloise or Nathan. So we took a pair of Eloise's earrings and shoved one through the ear. Scott dropped it on the path to the shed for you to find, and Courtney took the other earring and left it in Zen's house when he was confronting you on the roof."

"And the three of you took Nathan to the basement after we'd brought Zen in for questioning," I said, filling in the blanks.

"It worked so well with the elk blood everywhere," she said. "I just wish I knew what happened to Eloise."

"Do you think she might still be hiding?" I asked. "Trying to get Garrett's attention?"

She shook her head. "Before Nathan died, he said she wasn't supposed to move. That she planned on you finding her and then telling Garrett and Garrett would realize he loved her."

"But when I got back there with Garrett, she was gone," I said.

"Exactly," Bernadette said. "Someone else probably saw her and thought she was dead, or nearly dead, so they finished the job and disposed of her body."

"But who?" I asked. "And where would they have put her body?"

Bernadette sniffled. "I've been asking myself those same questions this entire time."

I thought about it for a moment. If Bernadette, Scott, and Courtney were together and Garrett was with me. That left my family, the wedding party, Zen, and a handful of staff still at the resort.

I didn't want to consider my family. I knew them. They wouldn't do anything like that.

Even though Megan was up and about. I was sure she had a perfectly reasonable explanation for where she was.

Maybe Hugo or Cedric could have done it. Neither of them seemed thrilled she was there. Selena was probably with the baby the entire time, and the nanny had nothing to do with anything.

Zen seemed an unlikely suspect, though he hated Eloise.

"Do you think Nathan put that necklace in my room after all?" I asked.

"I think when he realized she might actually have died, he needed to cover up any involvement he might have had with it. Implicating you only made sense." Bernadette narrowed her eyes at me. "You didn't hurt her, did you?"

I shook my head. "Do you think I'd be doing this much digging if I did?"

I could understand why she would have thought I had something to do with it. I was the last one to see her alive, if unconscious.

A thought popped into my head. "Come with me." I grabbed Bernadette's hand and pulled her back to the Den.

Garrett and Courtney sat in silence, both of their heads turning toward the door as we walked in.

"Garrett, do you remember the name of the shelter we were going to get our new puppy from?" I asked. "It slipped my mind."

"Puppy?" Garrett stood. "I didn't think we were getting a new puppy."

"Okay," I said. "And what about Fritz? Do you like him?"

"Rylie, are you okay?" Garrett asked.

Bernadette and Courtney watched in confusion.

"Just answer the question," I said. "What about Fritz? He's a good cat, right?"

Garrett pushed a hand against my head. "Do you have a fever? Are you delirious?"

"Answer. The. Question." I pushed his hand away.

"I don't know who Fritz is," Garrett said. "Fizzy is your dog—a very good one. But you don't have a cat."

I sighed in relief. "I thought maybe—"

"I was Derrick?" Recognition spread over his face. "And if I was Derrick, maybe I did something to Eloise."

"Is there any way Derrick could be here?" I asked.

"I'm pretty certain he didn't escape a maximum-security prison. As soon as we have service, I'll call to make sure." He paused. "But, even if he did escape, he liked Eloise."

Of course, he did.

Derrick had kidnapped me, yet he liked Eloise.

I was getting tired of feeling like second best to a woman who was missing or possibly even dead.

"Did she fess up to what she and Scott did?" I asked.

Courtney turned and glared at Bernadette. "What did you tell her?"

Bernadette shrugged. "The truth. I wasn't about to take the fall for the two of you murderers."

Garrett turned to Courtney. "Please tell me you didn't hurt Eloise."

"Why do you care? You're getting married to homely Rylie, remember?"

Garrett looked murderous.

"She didn't hurt Eloise," I said. "She and Scott killed Nathan because she saw Nathan hurt Eloise."

"Courtney," Garrett said, sinking into the chair across from her. "You can't kill people."

"I'd do anything to protect Eloise," she said. "He said he didn't hurt her, but I know he did. I saw him."

"Maybe he didn't," I said. "Maybe this was all a big scheme Eloise had planned to get Garrett back that went horribly wrong."

"Don't bad mouth Eloise when she's not here to stand up for herself," Courtney said.

"You and I both know Eloise could perfectly enact such a scheme," Bernadette said.

"Which one of you was she arguing with in the hallway after she and Nathan fought outside our rehearsal dinner?" I asked.

"Not me," Bernadette said. "You saw when I arrived well after all of that happened."

"It was me," Courtney said.

"What were you arguing about?" Garrett asked, his voice gentle.

"She wanted to get you back, so I told her just to march right in there and ask flat out. She said she couldn't. That it had to be your choice." Courtney looked down at her nicely manicured nails. "Then she told me to forget it and that she was going home."

"But she didn't go home," Garrett said.

We sat in silence for a minute.

"I need to talk to Zen," I said. "Garrett, can you wait here with Courtney? Scott ran off, but the police will definitely arrest her."

"What do you want me to do?" Bernadette asked.

"Go to the front desk and get some paper," I said. "Write down everything you just told me in as much detail as possible."

Zen was once again asleep in the room where Hugo stood watch.

"Wake up," Hugo said, his voice booming.

Zen sat up in a hurry and ran a hand through his hair. "Did you find her?"

"We have information about what happened to Eloise," I said, glancing up to see if Hugo gave any indication of surprise. He just looked bored. "But I'm here because we don't think you had anything to do with what happened to her."

Zen stood and threw his arms around my neck. "Does that mean I can go home?"

"Unfortunately, no," I said. "Your lizards are fine, but we found something in the basement."

"The elk?" Zen pulled away and looked at me with confusion. "I already told you it was down there."

"Yes, the elk," I said. "But also, Nathan. He's dead. In your basement."

Zen looked like he might faint. "I-I didn't—"

"We know," I said. "We already know who did. They were trying to frame you but did an atrocious job."

"Who did it?" Hugo asked.

"I'm not going to reveal anything until the police get here," I said. "But does the code PV222 or DV222 mean anything to you?"

He shook his head. "We have a room 222, but none of the buildings are labeled with letters.

Frustration crept through me. "Gah. If only we could get a line out to the police. They should be taking care of this."

Zen slapped himself on the forehead. "I don't know why I didn't think of it before. Maybe because I was being accused of murder."

"Think of what?" I asked.

"Blake has a radio that connects to the ones we use around here," he said. "If she's in her house or has it on her, we might be able to talk to her. And she might be able to call her mom."

That would have been incredibly helpful to know two days ago.

27

Zen hurried to the front desk and asked Carly to try Blake on the radio.

Everything moved really fast after that.

Blake answered and told us they were just getting the road cleared and that the police would be here soon.

Carly told her to keep an eye out for Scott while they were at it.

"Has anyone seen Devin?" Tom asked when he came out of the elevator. "He seems to have gone missing during an especially tough game of hide-and-seek."

"Have you checked your air vent?" I asked as something in my brain clicked into place. I hurried down the stairs and ran down the hallway toward the women's locker room.

Garrett ran after me. "What's up? Are you okay?"

I didn't have time to explain. If what I was thinking was right, Eloise might have hidden in plain sight all this time.

The air vent cover wasn't even screwed on. How had I not thought to look inside the air vent?

I pulled the cover off, expecting the worst. But was mildly disappointed when it was empty.

"Did you think Devin hid in the air vent again?" Garrett asked, peeking around me.

I shook my head. "I thought maybe Eloise hid in here. If she were going for the dramatic effect, it would make sense. It was close, and she could have easily fit with her tiny frame."

"But she's not in there," Garrett said.

"Not anymore." I pulled out my phone and pressed on the flashlight app. The light illuminated the inside of the vent. "But I think she was." I pointed to a smear of blood on the back of the vent. "And look at this, it looks like a piece of her black dress got caught here and ripped."

Garrett looked closer. "It makes sense. But if she was in there, where is she now?"

"Room 222," I said. "That's what the code stood for on Nathan's hand."

Garrett looked confused.

"It was their game plan," I said. "He was in on this whole thing from the beginning. P for pool. V for vent. And I bet if we go to room 222, we'll find Eloise."

Garrett and I didn't stick around to think about the validity of the plan.

In a flash, we were at the stairs, climbing them like our lives depended on it.

When we reached the second floor, Garrett yanked the door open and charged through it.

He got to the door first and pounded on it. "Eloise?"

The door flung open, and Eloise said, "It's about time you got here, Nath—oh! Garrett?"

I came into view.

"And Rylie? Why are you here? How did you know I was here?" Eloise wore expensive yoga pants and a cropped tank with her hair wrapped up in a bun on top of her head.

"We know everything," I said.

I looked at Garrett, but instead of backing me up, he wrapped Eloise in a big hug, his body heaving with sobs.

Eloise was too surprised to give me a gloating look.

"I'm so glad you're okay," Garrett said. "I thought you were dead."

She giggled. "I'm not. I'm fine. Did Nathan tell you? I knew I wasn't paying him enough to keep it quiet."

Garrett finally pulled away and looked down at her. "Nathan's dead."

Eloise looked back and forth between us in shock. "Dead? No, he's not. He's in his room. The room I paid for."

"Courtney and Scott killed him because they thought he hurt you."

"I told Courtney I had a plan, though," Eloise said, her voice shaky. "She told me not to, but I had to make one last effort."

"Why didn't you just talk to me?" Garrett asked.

"I've tried," Eloise said. "I didn't think you'd realize how much you loved me until you'd lost me."

Garrett looked like he might say something else, but instead, he turned and walked away down the hall.

We watched as he pushed the door to the stairwell

open with so much force, the banging echoed down the hall.

"I'd say that went well," Eloise said.

I looked at her in disgust. "Well? How do you figure? Nathan is dead. Because of your little stunt."

"I didn't kill him."

"You might as well have."

"He knew the dangers when I hired him."

"He knew you had a sister capable of murder? Are you sure?"

"He told her to leave when he saw us," she said. "I was there."

"Then you hid in the vent after I saw you?"

"I thought you could use some excitement being trapped inside this entire time."

"No," I said. "You wanted to ruin any chance of me getting married."

She shrugged. "That too."

"I'm through with this," I said. "The police will be here shortly. I'm sure they'll want to talk to you."

"Why? I did nothing wrong."

"Pretending to get attacked is pretty wrong, maybe even criminal," I said. "But I'll leave that up to them. In fact, I'm done with solving crimes. I'm going to leave that to the police from now on too."

I walked away without looking back.

The police were in the lobby when I got back downstairs. One of the officers held tight to Scott's arm.

"Rylie," Blake said. "Are you okay?"

"I'm fine," I said. "Have you seen Garrett?"

She shook her head. "He didn't come through here."

I'd have to find him.

Did I want to find him?

What if he had changed his mind about our wedding?

I'd have to face the facts, eventually.

For now, I had a lot of explaining to do so the police could take the investigation over.

It took hours to tell the police everything. We walked through the crime verbally and then physically. I showed them where I'd found Eloise's body, where she'd hidden in the vent, all the way to Zen's cabin, and finally to room 222.

By the time they had all the information, I was completely wrecked. I needed to sleep in a bad way.

But as I was sneaking off to my room, Megan grabbed me by the arm. "There's something I need to show you."

"Please, please, please don't let it be a body or a body part or anything having to do with crime."

She didn't say anything.

When we got to the den, a whole gaggle of people shouted, "Surprise!"

Fizzy nearly knocked me over with his big paws and even bigger kisses.

As I hugged him tight around his neck, I realized everyone was here. Shayla and Seamus, Nikki and a guy that looked vaguely familiar, all the guys from work, Garrett's mom, and several people I didn't recognize that I assumed were from Garrett's side of the family.

"How?" I asked, still trying to get my tired brain wrapped around what was going on.

"The roads cleared," Shayla said, giving me a big hug. "You can get married after all!"

But as I looked around, one key element was missing —Garrett.

I needed to talk to him. He'd been so overwhelmed with emotion when he'd found out Eloise was alive, I wasn't certain how he'd feel about going forward with the wedding.

But I didn't have the heart to tell our friends and family that. Not just yet.

"I'm so happy you're here," I said. "Thank you for taking extra time to wait out the storm."

"We wouldn't miss this for the world," Greg—my boss and Ranger One—said, wrapping me up in a grandfatherly hug.

Blake walked in and smiled. "I know not all of you have rooms reserved. However, we are happy to accommodate anyone who needs a room so we can make this wedding happen tomorrow. If you need accommodations, please head over to the front desk, and Carly will get you all set up."

Several people walked out of the room, many of them hugging me on their way by.

"Where is Garrett?" Blake asked quietly.

"I'm not sure," I said. "He was pretty torn up about the whole Eloise thing. I think he might be in shock."

"Do you think he's going to back out of the wedding?" Megan asked.

"I have no idea," I said. "But I should probably try to find him and see what he thinks."

"Do you want us to go with you?" Shayla asked, grabbing my hand.

"This is something I need to do by myself." I squeezed her hand. "But thank you."

"Once you're finished with Garrett, call me, okay?" Megan said.

"I'm pretty tired. Can I call you in the morning?" I asked.

"I just want to know what happened," she said. "Plus, wouldn't it be best to tell everyone if the wedding won't happen tomorrow before you just don't show up?"

She had a point. "Okay, I'll call you." I looked at Shayla. "Both of you."

Shayla smiled. "I'm sure the wedding will be on, and everything will be perfect."

I could only hope so. "Come on, Fizzy." He followed me as I made my way to confront my destiny.

———

Garrett wasn't in his room.

Or outside with Babbitt.

Or anywhere I could find.

I even checked Eloise's original room and room 222—both were empty.

My steps were heavy, but my heart was heavier.

What if he'd simply left?

I checked my phone to see if he'd responded to my text message.

It said he'd read it over an hour ago.

But I hadn't seen so much as three dots indicating he was typing a message in reply.

I arrived at my room and walked inside, fully intending on texting Megan and Shayla before passing out on the bed.

Much to my surprise, Megan, Shayla, and a bunch of other women were huddled in my bedroom wearing skimpy bikinis, brightly colored feather boas, and party hats.

"How did it go?" Megan asked, meeting me at the door. "You were supposed to text me."

"What is all of this?" I asked.

"Your bachelorette party," Megan said.

"But you don't even know if the wedding is happening," I said.

"I guess, we assumed," she said. "Wait. Is it not?"

"I couldn't find Garrett," I said. "He won't respond to my text messages or anything."

"Maybe he's trying to keep with tradition," Shayla said. "You know, no contact with the bride the night before the wedding?"

My eyes felt like they were either going to explode with tears or slam shut.

"Here," Megan said, pushing a large energy drink into my hand. "Drink this. Tonight, we're going to party. We'll deal with tomorrow when tomorrow comes."

Everyone looked so excited.

All I wanted to do was lay in my bed and cry.

But I couldn't ruin this for them.

Or for myself.

If I did get married tomorrow, I'd regret not participating in my bachelorette party.

And I needed to think positively.

Garrett had been telling me this entire time that he still wanted to marry me. Why would I assume any different?

I smiled. "Okay, let's do this."

The women squealed and shouted.

"First thing's first," Nikki said. "We need to get you dressed."

The women's locker room looked as if nothing had recently happened. Shayla assured me the police had cleared the scene.

When I walked into the pool area, my eyes nearly popped out of my head.

Not only was the entire room lit up with flashing lights and disco balls, but a whole gaggle of hot guys in banana hammocks stood ready to wait on us.

"We have a mani-pedi station," Megan yelled over the bass-heavy music. "A massage station, a lap dance station, a dance floor, all the drinks you could ever want, and tons of food. This is your last night of freedom. Live it up."

I gaped at her. "What about you? You're a married woman."

"Tom doesn't mind," she said. "Plus, he lost our kid today. He owes me."

"Did you find him?"

"Fizzy did," she said. "He was hiding in the den behind the drapes."

I'd left Fizzy in my hotel room, but at the mention of him, the urge to squeeze his neck overwhelmed me. I'd have to make sure I cuddled him a bunch after this party was over.

"What are you waiting for?" Nikki said. "Let's get this party started!"

Mr. Nothing-But-Abs manning the DJ booth turned the music up. Nikki, Shayla, and Megan cheered. I joined along.

I'd probably skip the lap dance station, but all the others sounded amazing.

A guy with a man bun and a five o'clock shadow handed me a drink. "The Rylie for Rylie," he said in a deep voice. "Can I get you anything else?"

I took a sip and savored it. "I think I'll start with a pedicure and some food." My stomach grumbled. I hadn't eaten since breakfast in the den with Garrett. Had that been just this morning? It was amazing how much could change in a day.

Shayla joined me at the pedicure station, sitting in the chair next to me, while Nikki, Logan, Megan, and some of the others headed out to the dance floor. I admired their complete lack of inhibition dancing in bikinis in front of a bunch of random hot men.

I looked down at my stomach and sighed. I'd wanted abs before my wedding day—or at least some definition.

"Stop picking yourself apart," Shayla said. "You're perfect."

"Me?" I asked. "Look at you. You've been working out, haven't you?"

Shayla blushed. When I'd first met her, she was so self-conscious. "I guess I finally lost the freshman fifteen."

"You're beautiful now, and you were beautiful before," I said.

"Thanks," she said. "That's what Seamus said too."

"Speaking of Seamus, are the two of you still heading to Ireland for the holidays?"

Shayla smiled. "That's the plan."

"He's totally going to propose," I said. "Are you ready? What are you going to say?"

"I'm going to say yes, duh!" She laughed. "Assuming he proposes. Maybe this is just a trip to meet his parents. He hasn't done any prep work in asking what kind of rings I like or anything."

I considered this. He hadn't asked me for advice on the ring front either. Maybe he wasn't going to propose.

"Either way," she said. "It'll be a fun trip. I'm beyond excited to meet his family."

"And Ireland at Christmas?" I smiled. "It sounds wonderful. What if you don't want to come home?"

"Don't worry about that," she said. "I'll be back."

"That's good," I said. "I don't know what I'd do if I lost another friend."

"Another friend?" Shayla asked, then took a sip of her drink.

"Luke," I said. "You know, part of me thought he'd make it to the wedding."

"Why?" Shayla said. "So he could watch the woman he's been in love with for years marry another man?"

I could feel my jaw drop open.

"Oh, come on, you know it as well as I do," she said.

I shook my head. "He had a chance to date me, and he turned me down."

"That was right after you got out of a relationship with Troy," she said. "He was protecting himself."

"From me?"

"Aren't you the one who broke his heart in front of your entire graduating class?"

"But we were kids," I said. "He couldn't have thought I'd really marry him that early in our lives."

She shrugged. "It doesn't matter now, does it? You're marrying Garret,t and he's in another country."

"And he dated Nikki," I said. "Which means he's over me."

"If that's what you need to tell yourself, then go right ahead." She motioned over at Nikki. "Did you see who she brought as her date?"

"I saw him, but I couldn't place him."

"It's naked guy," she said, laughter brightening her face. "They've been dating for a while, apparently."

"That's crazy," I said with a laugh. Who would have thought Nikki would date the guy we often had arrested for running around the park in the nude? "Oh, and thanks for looking after Fizzy and Babbitt. I hope they were good for you."

"They were angels," she said. "As always. You know, I don't know who I'll miss more around the apartment—you or Fizzy."

"Fizzy," I said. "Definitely Fizzy."

"You're probably right," she said, then reached over and grabbed my hand. "Can you believe you're getting married tomorrow? You're going to be like a real-life adult.”

"It's crazy," I said. "But I'm excited."

I couldn't help but wonder if it was actually going to happen.

3 0

By the time the sun was peeking up over the horizon, I was covered in body oil, glitter, sweat, and a couple of feathers from the boas. My nails and toes had been painted, and my head spun from too much alcohol.

Thankfully, we had planned an evening wedding, and I'd be able to sleep most of the day.

I showered and changed into my comfiest pajamas before sliding into bed.

Megan hadn't allowed anyone to bring their phones to the bachelorette party. That way, there was no evidence. I hesitantly picked mine up from the nightstand to check if I had any messages.

Nothing.

I knew the superstition about not seeing the bride before the wedding, but a simple text confirming the wedding was on would have been nice.

I sighed. I was too tired to think about it any more than I already had.

I woke to my mother knocking on the door. "How's my little bride-to-be?" She slid her card and walked in without my approval. "Oh my! You look awful!"

"I just woke up," I groaned. "Give me a break."

"We don't have all day," she said. "Let's get moving."

She insisted I shower again—saying I smelled like alcohol—even though I'd just showered a few hours before.

I wouldn't admit it to her, but the shower did help wake me up.

"The hairstylist and makeup artist are downstairs. Are you ready?"

"Have you heard from Garrett?" I snuck a peek at my phone. Still no messages.

"Why would I need to hear from Garrett?"

"There's a chance he might not want to go through with the wedding after what happened with Eloise."

"That's absurd." Mom pushed me out the door and toward the elevators. "Garrett loves you. If he didn't want to marry you, he wouldn't have proposed a second time after you kissed that other man."

She had a way of hitting me where it hurt most.

"That was almost a year ago," I said. "You should have seen him hug Eloise when he found out she was alive."

"He was probably just relieved," Mom said. "Don't think twice about it."

I was definitely thinking twice and thrice and so forth about it.

"If it helps, I'll check in with his mother to see if all is well."

"Would you?" I asked.

She wrapped an arm around my shoulder and kissed me on the head. "I'd do anything for you, sweetheart." The doors to the elevator opened, and Mom pulled me out. "Now, let's get a move on."

Before I knew it, my hair was curled and situated to cover the bald spots, my makeup was near-perfection, and my dress was hoisted over my head, the lace coming to rest on my shoulders and back.

I did my best not to itch at the fabric. The seamstress had warned me how fragile the lace could be, and with the new daggers I had on my fingertips, I'd surely rip it.

Mom secured the veil on top of my head, and everyone stood back to admire me.

"You're stunning," Mom said.

"Absolutely gorgeous," Shayla agreed.

Megan wiped a tear from her eye. "Garrett's a lucky guy."

I turned to glance in the full-length mirror.

I looked so much older and different. Prettier. More done up. Exactly as I suspected I would from the moment I accepted Garrett's second proposal.

Butterflies flapped in my chest as the music began to play.

"That's our cue," Zen said, entering the room. "You look breathtaking. Are you ready?"

"Wait." I grabbed Mom before she could walk out of the room. "Did Garrett's mom say he'd be there?"

"He's there," Zen said. "Waiting for you."

A sigh of relief escaped my lips. "Great, then I'm ready."

My bridesmaids, all dressed in sleek black dresses holding pink roses, followed Zen and my mother out of the room. Fizzy was next, but he stopped right in front of me and started heaving like he did when he ate too much grass.

"Fizzy, no," I said.

But it was too late.

Whatever he had gotten into—something yellowish-green—was now all over the carpet and the bottom of my dress.

"Are you okay?" I bent down to pet Fizzy.

He wagged his tail.

"Your dress!" Zen shouted.

Everyone in the hall turned to look.

Mom flew into action. "Nothing a little cold water can't fix."

"Looks like you and I both had some butterflies, huh?"

I narrowly missed one of Fizzy's big kisses. "Oh no you don't," I said. "This makeup took too long for you to go messing it up with your puke slobber."

"There," Mom said. "Good as new."

"Sorry about the carpet," I said to Zen.

"That's neither here nor there," he said. "We'll get it all taken care of. Now, you get your butt down that aisle before your groom changes his mind."

Mom gave Zen a dirty look.

"Not that he will," Zen said.

I stood back up. "Ready, Fizz?"

He turned in a circle.

"No more barfing, okay?"

He barked loudly.

Zen jumped about a foot in the air.

Mom hurried back to the front of the group while Zen helped me over the spot in the carpet, so the rest of my dress didn't drag in the vomit.

My dad was standing just outside the door, and when I saw the look on his face, tears welled in my eyes.

"Don't make me cry," I whispered. "I'll ruin all this makeup."

"Me make you cry?" Dad laughed. "What about ruining my makeup? That would be even more embarrassing."

I glanced up to see if he was truly wearing makeup. He smiled. "Gotcha."

I laughed and blinked the tears away.

"You sure about this, kiddo?" Dad asked.

"Why do you ask?"

The music started, and the bridesmaids were walking down the aisle. I couldn't see Garrett over their heads, but I assumed if he wasn't up there, they wouldn't be moving.

"I overheard you talking about how much this wedding cost your mother and me, and I never want you to think losing money is worth sacrificing your happiness."

I smiled. "Noted. Thanks, Dad."

It was almost my turn. I'd walk up that aisle and marry the man I loved.

I sucked in a deep breath as the music changed.

"Here we go," Dad said.

We walked up the aisle exactly as Zen had instructed.

When I looked up from my feet, I saw Garrett. He was looking down, almost as if he was praying.

His suit fit him perfectly. He was a gorgeous man.

And when he looked up and smiled, all of my worries evaporated.

The butterflies flew away.

I glanced around at the people in the room.

Garrett's family and friends on one side, mine on the other.

Every eye watched me.

As I passed by, Seamus, Dusty, Greg, and Ben smiled. Antonio barely looked at me.

Naked guy—thankfully not naked at the moment—sat with Logan and Eli. Logan still looked a bit hungover from the night before. It served her right. She and Nikki had probably done at least a half dozen shots each. I chuckled to myself at the thought of them trying to dance in their bikinis and boas.

Mom's eyes were misty as I approached, but she quickly wiped the tears away so as not to ruin her makeup.

Megan, Shayla, and Nikki stood at the front of the church across from Cedric and Hugo. Noticeably missing was Scott, but if you didn't know he was supposed to be there, it probably wouldn't have been as noticeable other than the asymmetrical sides.

"Who gives this woman to be married today?" the tiny old pastor asked.

"Her mother and I do," Dad said, lifting my veil and kissing me on the cheek.

We'd had to discuss whether Dad would lift the veil or

Garrett after we were married. In the end, we settled on Dad doing it.

I walked up the steps to come face to face with Garrett.

He smiled, and I smiled back.

"Dearly beloved," the pastor started, "we are gathered here today to join this man and woman in holy matrimony.

"Do you, Garrett, take Rylie to be your lawfully wedded wife? To have and to hold from this day forward? For better or for worse? For richer or for poorer? In sickness and in health? As long as you both shall live?"

Garrett nodded at the pastor. "I do."

"And do you, Rylie, take Garrett to be your lawfully wedded wife? To have and to hold from this day forward? For better or for worse? For richer or for poorer? In sickness and in health? As long as you both shall live?"

I smiled at Garrett. "I do."

Garrett nodded again.

"The word of God tells us what love is like and what love does," the pastor continued. "Love is patient . . ."

I'd been very patient the past couple of days. Especially with Eloise's reappearance.

"Love is kind. Love is not jealous."

Oof, we both had that one against us. I tried to meet Garrett's eye, but he had his gaze trained on the pastor.

"Love does not brag and is not arrogant. It does not act unbecomingly."

I mean, not responding to my text messages the night before our wedding and making me wonder whether he'd be at the ceremony the next day was a bit unbecoming.

"It does not seek its own, it is not easily provoked, and it does not hold grudges."

Garrett definitely hadn't held a grudge against Eloise when he found out she was alive.

". . . for love bears all things, believes all things, hopes all things, and endures all things, but above all, love never fails."

My stomach twisted.

Garrett had failed me. Over and over again since Eloise came back into the picture.

And even before that. He'd lied to me.

He should have told me about Eloise trying to get in touch with him.

"Having this love in your hearts for one another, you have chosen to exchange rings as the sign and seal of the vows you are making to one another today." The pastor reached for the rings Cedric was holding out to him. "But before we do that, I'd like to ask if anyone has an objection to this marriage?"

Garrett and I both turned to look at the pastor.

We hadn't scripted this. We'd intentionally left it out.

Our wedding day was not to be at the mercy of someone who wanted to mess it up.

Someone cleared their throat loudly in the back of the room.

Every head turned to see who it was.

My heart raced.

Was it Antonio? Was that why he hadn't looked at me?

Or Luke? Was Luke there?

"Did someone in the back have something to say?" the pastor asked.

No one moved. The room was so silent, you could hear Devin twisting in his chair.

"I guess if no one is going to object, we will proceed with the rings."

Garrett and I turned to face each other again.

"Garrett, will you please take this ring, place it on the third finger of Rylie's hand, and repeat after me: with this ring, I thee wed."

Garrett didn't move.

He didn't reach for the ring.

Even when the pastor pushed his open hand up against Garrett's arm, Garrett remained stiff as a statue.

"Garrett?" I whispered.

The second Garrett's gaze met mine, I knew.

"It's okay," I said.

Garrett swallowed, his Adam's apple dancing in his throat.

I reached for his hands. "We don't have to do this."

A single tear fell from his eye. "I made a promise to you. A promise I want to keep."

I pulled my engagement ring off my finger and slipped it into his palm. "You don't have to keep this one. It's okay."

"But—"

I shook my head. "No buts. This is the rest of our lives we're talking about. If we're not one million percent sure—"

Garrett winced. As an accountant, he hated when I said a number higher than one hundred percent.

"Sorry," I said. "But if we're not completely certain that this is what we want, we shouldn't do this."

"Are you completely certain?" Garrett asked.

"You know, I thought I was, but now I'm not so sure."

Garrett squeezed my hand. "I love you, Rylie."

"And I love you."

He brought my hand to his lips and kissed it.

My dad stood as Garrett started back down the aisle alone.

For a second, I thought Dad might punch Garrett. But he held out a hand. "Thank you for making such a hard decision," Dad said.

Garrett shook his hand. "I'll send you a check for the wedding."

"That's completely unnecessary," Dad said.

"Consider it done," Garrett said. "I'm so sorry."

Dad nodded, and Garrett looked back one last time at me before running out the door, Babbitt chasing after him.

The sound of the door closing sent everything into motion.

Chaos erupted. Fizzy barked obnoxiously. People swarmed, trying to make sure I was okay. Several people ran after Garrett.

A whistle from the back of the room made everyone stop.

A man stood in the doorway.

"What the hell happened?" Zen bellowed. "I was so close. Go after him. Get him back here."

No one moved.

"Zen, it's okay," I said. "This is for the best."

"The best for who? Not me!" Zen looked frantic. "I needed this wedding."

Blake stood from the back of the room. "Zen, you and I can discuss this another time."

Zen looked like he wanted to discuss it now, but Blake gave him a warning look.

Zen turned and stormed out of the room.

"Now," Blake said, taking control of the situation. "If everyone would follow me to the reception hall. We don't want a good party to go to waste, do we?"

I smiled, thankful for Blake.

"You heard the woman. Let's party!" Megan linked her arm in mine, and we made our way back up the aisle, everyone following behind.

As we passed the dressing room, I had an overwhelming urge to rip off my dress. "You go ahead," I said. "I have something I need to do."

She stared me down for a minute, then nodded. "Promise you won't just go back to your room?"

"I promise," I said.

She left, calling Fizzy to follow her, while I took a detour to the dressing room.

Zen wasn't lying. The staff had already gotten the carpet completely clean from Fizzy's puking incident.

I couldn't get the lace off any faster than I did without ripping it. Sure, it had a cleaned-up puke stain on it, but someone might still buy it secondhand.

As the dress came off my shoulders, so did a weight. I hadn't realized how heavy the wedding had been weighing on me.

Had it been because of Eloise that I felt this way? Or had I known Garrett wasn't the one for me but had been ignoring it?

I suspected it was the latter.

As I stood in my bra and underwear, I realized I'd worn yoga pants and a tank top under my silky white bridal robe when I'd come to get dressed. I had nothing else to wear.

A knock at the door had me ducking for cover.

"Oh, come on," Mom said. "How many times do I have to tell you? I made you, birthed you—"

"And bathed you," I finished. "I know. I thought you might be someone else."

"Like who?" Mom asked. "Pretty sure everyone is at your reception right now."

"So why are you here?"

"I wanted to make sure you had something to wear," she said. "I was going to give you this to take on your honeymoon, but I figured you might want it now instead."

She handed me a zipped-up bag.

"Thank you," I said.

"I'll see you at the party." She closed the door with one last smile.

I opened the bag and gasped. The floor-length pink dress had spaghetti straps and what looked like a daring side slit, but not a single piece of lace.

I slipped it over my head and smiled at the slit that came halfway up my thigh.

From the look of the dress, Garrett had been planning to take me somewhere warm for our honeymoon.

A knock on the door made me smile.

"Yes, Mom?" I laughed.

"Uh, sorry, not Mom," the voice said. "Are you decent?"

"Yes," I said, trying to keep my heart rate in check.

It couldn't possibly be who I thought it was.

But when he came around the corner, my knees went weak.

Luke.

"What are you doing here?" I asked.

"I came to support you," he said.

"Support my marriage? Or—"

"You." He shrugged and leaned against the door frame. "Just you. Whatever you chose to do."

Tears spilled over onto my cheeks. Luke looked gorgeous in khaki pants and a nice sweater with a button-down shirt layered underneath. "I didn't think you'd be able to make it."

"As much as it would have hurt to see you marry someone else, I wanted to be here for you." He looked me up and down. "You look gorgeous, by the way."

I laughed. "My makeup is probably all smeared now."

"Makeup? You don't need makeup," he said. "But maybe you do need a hug?"

He opened his arms.

My feet couldn't carry me fast enough to fall into them.

His hug made everything better.

"I'm so sorry this happened," he said. "I can't imagine how you feel right now."

I cried into his chest, letting every emotion I'd bottled up flow out of me.

Luke held me in silence until I could compose myself.

I took a step back and looked up into his eyes.

He wiped the tears from my face. "How about we get you to your party? I'm sure everyone wants to know how you're holding up."

"Do I look terrible?"

"Far from it."

"Thank you for coming," I said.

He smiled and kissed me on the forehead. "Thank you for not marrying Garrett."

Want to know what Garrett, Luke, and Antonio were thinking during the wedding? Check out the FREE short story—*In His Eyes*—from their points of view.

To get your short story, go to:
    https://BookHip.com/SWZMQBA

Thank you so much for reading *Snowed*!

Don't miss the next book in the Rylie Cooper Series—*Wasted*. Preorder your copy today!

I would be honored and eternally grateful if you would post a review on Amazon, Bookbub, and/or Goodreads about the book.

Also, I love hearing from readers! Email me at stellabixbyauthor@gmail.com.

XOXO,

Stella Bixby

ACKNOWLEDGMENTS

My hometown played such an integral part of the creation of Big Mountain. Granby, Colorado is a beautiful place to visit and was a wonderful place to call home. Thank you, Granby.

I want to thank all of my readers. When I started this journey, I never thought I'd have so many. Now, I couldn't imagine writing these books without a single one of you. Your messages, emails, likes, reviews, and comments keep me motivated to write the next book. That's why this book is dedicated to you.

Thank you to my family, my friends, my betas, my arc team, and God (in no particular order). I am so thankful for each of you.

ABOUT THE AUTHOR

Stella Bixby is a native Coloradan who loves to snowboard, pluck at the guitar, and play board games with her family. She was once a volunteer firefighter and a park ranger, but now spends most of her time making up stories and trying to figure out what to cook for dinner.

Connect with Stella on Facebook, Twitter, and Instagram @StellaBixby.

Stella loves to hear from her readers!
www.stellabixby.com

Novels:

Rylie Cooper Series

Catfished: Book 1

Suckered: Book 2

Throttled: Book 3

Tampered: Book 4

Whacked: Book 5

Bungled: Book 6

Snowed: Book 7

Magical Mane Mystery Series

Downward Death: Book 1

Bowling Blunder: Book 2

Spotlight Scandal: Book 3

Tango Trouble: Book 4

Spelunking Speculations: Book 5

Festival Fiasco: Book 6

www.ingramcontent.com/pod-product-compliance
Lightning Source LLC
Chambersburg PA
CBHW030401200726

48286CB00015B/2410